# JOURNEY INTO DARKNESS

---

## *An American in Hitler's Wehrmacht*

---

Lowell W. Culver

**Hamilton Books**
an imprint of
**University Press of America,® Inc.**
*Lanham • Boulder • New York • Toronto • Plymouth, UK*

**Copyright © 2014 by**
**Hamilton Books**
4501 Forbes Boulevard
Suite 200
Lanham, Maryland 20706
Hamilton Books Acquisitions Department (301) 459-3366

10 Thornbury Road
Plymouth PL6 7PP
United Kingdom

British Library Cataloging in Publication Information Available

Library of Congress Control Number: 2013951266
ISBN: 978-0-7618-6245-1 (paperback
eISBN: 978-0-7618-6246-8

*To the Memory of My Mother,*

*Lanie Jensen Culver,*

*Who Gave Me the Heritage*

*That Made This Book Possible*

# CONTENTS

# Preface

History is replete with examples of populations being mobilized and manipulated to achieve the personal and often perverted goals of an ambitious national leadership. Nowhere has mastery over subjects been more fully realized than in the modern totalitarian state, with its monopoly over the instruments of force, control of communications and absence of political restraints. Taking advantage of the economic and political tumult of the early 1930s and of the frustrations of the German people, Adolf Hitler, by offering hope, order from chaos, identification with a dynamic enterprise and national dignity through removal of the perceived humiliation imposed by the Treaty of Versailles, gained a sufficient following to be handed the reins of government in January, 1933. Drawing on his initial base of fanatical supporters, particularly youth, who considered him as a savior of the German nation, he quickly suppressed all opposition and extended his control over the German state, with full power to engage the energies of its people along lines determined by the National Socialist movement.

Relying at first on bluff and bravado to alter existing arrangements, the new Germany soon turned to open threats as it gained in military strength. When measures short of war failed to achieve desired ends, as in the case of Danzig and the Polish Corridor, the German leader, ignoring the desires of most Germans for a peaceful resolution of differences, resorted to armed aggression, convinced that his gamble would bring swift and relatively painless victory and that the British and French would not honor their pledge to Poland. While each victory gave his subjects new hope for peace, Hitler saw in them a new reason for more ambitious ventures, and the German masses were commandeered as marionettes in a puppet show to satisfy his megalomaniac thirst for power. When, in the end, it became clear that he had overreached himself, rather than suing for peace to stop the slaughter, he opted for a policy of national suicide. If his regime had to be destroyed, then, the German people should be destroyed with it. However blameworthy in making the Nazi terror state possible and bringing untold suffering to the peoples of Europe, the German masses also became tragic victims of the absurd goals of their depraved leadership.

Lest the deaths and maiming of countless millions on both sides in World War II be forgotten, let all the world be mindful of the perils of national leaderships for which there are no boundaries. The totalitarian appeal is often seductive in a world where answers to major problems are not always simple, where feelings of superfluousness are common in an overcrowded, atomized globe, and where political responsibility imposes special burdens not all are willing to bear. The lesson of the Hitler dictatorship is not just the moral abyss into which the German people allowed themselves to fall, but how human beings anywhere, under conditions of extreme stress, become capable of replicating the malevolence of the past.

Lowell W. Culver

# CHAPTER I

# A Fated Reunion

The purpose of my trip to Normandy was to meet several of my surviving buddies who had landed with me in the neighboring fields forty years earlier. As I drove across the Douve River and up the hill to Ste. Mère Eglise, my thoughts were drawn by the picturesque landscape of long, stone farm houses, neatly-spaced hedgerows and fruit orchards to that momentous day in June, 1944 when we were among those called upon to put our lives on the line to bring an end to the darkness which had covered continental Europe for four years. Then, the shrubbery and trees had been both a menace and a blessing, providing at once obstacles to our paratroops and landing glider craft and a protective covering to our otherwise exposed men. Now, other than the several war museums, including the one dedicated to the 82nd and 101st airborne divisions at Ste. Mère Eglise, and remnants of German fortifications in the dunes along the Varreville shoreline and on the heights at St. Marcouf, the countryside revealed few reminders of that earlier engagement.

While a lasting peace still seemed far away, at least the meeting provided a chance, perhaps the last for many of us, to reminisce about what had occurred there that day in Normandy. For me, June 6, 1944 had a special meaning, for it was the occasion of a reunion which was to change the course of my life.

## * June 1944 *

Shortly after 10:00 p.m. June 5 at our embarkation point in England we boarded the waiting C-47 troop transports which were to carry us to France to participate in the long-awaited assault on Hitler's Atlantic Wall. A personal visit earlier that day by General Eisenhower served to improve spirits; but most of us welcomed the order to embark, having undergone months of training and preparation and been confined to quarters for over a week.

Our unit was part of a larger American airborne force of some 13,000 paratroopers and supporting glider regiments which was to be landed behind enemy lines several hours prior to the anticipated arrival of the major invasion armada by sea. We were to carry out the extremely dangerous, but critical, mission of disrupting enemy communications, impeding the movement of reinforcements to the coastal invasion points, securing exits from the landing beaches and causing as much confusion as possible prior to the landings. Both we and the British, who were staging a like airborne operation east of Caen on the eastern flank of the 50-mile wide invasion front, hoped for a modicum of cooperation from French resistance fighters, farmers and small townspeople to help us accomplish our objectives. An attempt was made to select landing sites well away from heavily defended areas to allow time for our units to regroup before becoming engaged.

When fully outfitted, a parachutist could nearly double his weight and was a virtual walking arsenal, with rifle, pistol, assortment of knives, four blocks of T.N.T., six fragmentation grenades, ammunition and several specialty explosive devices to make him as self-sufficient as possible. He counted heavily on the division's glider group to reinforce him and his fellow troopers with equipment too heavy or bulky to carry in, such as anti-tank weapons, mortars, flame throwers and small vehicles.

A major air offensive had been directed against targets in northern France during April and May to cripple the region's transportation network and soften up German positions along the coast, and additional missions were flown early in the invasion morning. Later in the day we could count on support from the powerful guns of American and British naval vessels and an air cover of some 10,000 combat aircraft. The goal of the Allied High Command was to secure a beachhead and land up to 200,000 men within the first 24 hours and, ultimately, to bring ashore 600,000 men, comprised of 20 American, 17 British Empire, one Free French and one Free Polish divisions.

Our men were carried into battle by a vast fleet of khaki-painted C-47 transport aircraft, whose fuselages and wings were ringed by three broad white bands for easy identification. From the embarkation points in Southern England, the air armada flew in clear weather towards Brittany before turning sharply eastward into the Cotentin peninsula, where its various units were to jump into predetermined zones marked out by pathfinders who had parachuted in earlier. The drop zones were north of Carentan and from two to four miles inland from the beaches where the American VII Corps was to come ashore later in the morning.

Most of the men in our group came from the big cities of the Northeast and Midwest and represented a wide diversity of ethnic backgrounds. Three, other than myself, were of German extraction and could speak the language of the enemy. Two of us had seen duty in North Africa and Sicily with the 82nd Airborne division, but this would be the first test of battle for the rest of the men. What was lacking in seasoning was offset by the strong desire on the part of the men to bring the war home to Hitler and end the conflict as quickly as possible.

At 27 I was one of the older members of the unit and among those with the longest service record, having entered the Army just after Pearl Harbor. I had combat experience and, with the rank of Sergeant, was partially responsible for maintaining the spirits of the men as we moved into battle. In spite of intensive training in both the United States and England, we all experienced varying degrees of anxiety, for we knew that, given the nature of our mission, some of us would not survive the day. The possibility of being shot down by anti-aircraft fire or by German nightfighters or being killed after we left the plane compounded our fears. Yet, some in the plane were able to sleep; others smoked as if it would be their last, prayed or just stared ahead as if in a trance. There was little talking. As on other occasions when I felt overwhelmed by fear or grief, I sought refuge in the fourth verse of the 23rd Psalm and repeated it over and over again:

> "Yea, though I walk through the
> valley of the shadow of death, I will
> fear no evil: for Thou art with me;
> Thy rod and Thy staff they comfort me."

Partially reassured, I joined in with several of the men who were endeavoring to sing. It was dark in the plane with only a glimmer coming from the red light over the exit door. Then I turned to Beneš, the last to be assigned to our stick, and asked him where he was from.

"Chicago," came the reply.

"Did you know," I continued, "that you have the same family name as the former president of Czechoslovakia?"

"Yes, Sarge, but I don't think we are related. There wasn't any Czechoslovakia when my parents came to the States in 1908, and they never claimed a relationship."

"Well," I noted, "from what the Krauts did to your parents' homeland, you've got an additional score to settle when we get to France!"

Just then I overheard Moscowitz with one of his many jokes. Where he got them all is beyond me, but, for most of us, he was a godsend in helping to relieve the tension that was so obvious.

"John," I asked, "tell the one you told me the other day about Adolf Hitler."

"All right," he replied, "it goes something like this. Hitler, stopping at a small village in the Bavarian Alps known for its spectacular views, came across a little girl who looked very sad. Seemingly concerned, the Führer asked if there was anything he could do to cheer her up. Immediately recognizing the man who had addressed her from the many pictures she had seen of him, she said, hesitatingly, that she didn't want anything just for herself, but knew how he could make the whole world happy. 'How is that?' inquired the perplexed leader. 'By jumping off the cliff!' was the reply."

We all smiled and wished it would be that easy.

For me, participation in hostilities against German army units posed a special dilemma. My thoughts raced back to that day in July 1939, when I last saw my twin brother, Kurt, leaving on the German liner Bremen to study in Berlin. In spite of pleas by my parents for him to return home after the invasion of Poland, he decided to stick it out in anticipation of an eventual peaceful settlement. Peace never came, and shortly after the German move into Russia, he joined the Wehrmacht and never returned home. Our last communication concerning Kurt had been received in August, 1941 from the U.S. State Department, informing us that he had renounced his American citizenship and joined the German army. We had not heard from him since and did not know what happened to him.

Kurt had brought enormous grief to Mom and Dad by not returning home after the outbreak of war in 1939, or even later, when it appeared that the United States would eventually be drawn into the conflict. That grief was compounded by his decision to join the German cause. My decision to volunteer for the Army right after Pearl Harbor, rather than waiting to be drafted, was influenced as much by Kurt's behavior as by my own sense of duty. Mother could at least say that she had a son in the American armed forces, and this provided her with some psychological support, although she had no great desire to see me go off to war.

What if, through some crazy coincidence, my brother was still alive and had been assigned to the German divisions awaiting our invasion? With all the fronts on which the Germans were fighting, in Russia, Italy and now France, that seemed to be highly unlikely. Nevertheless, the notion of such a possibility haunted me throughout the flight. This had not been the case on any of my previous actions against the Germans.

But my thoughts were quickly turned to more immediate matters by the first sound of anti-aircraft fire as we skirted the French coast. Our low altitude and relatively slow speed made us extremely vulnerable, even with the partial darkness and the haze which had developed, and it was not surprising when several 20 millimeter shells ripped through the aircraft walls. The craft shook for a moment, throwing a number of us off balance, but the plane remained intact and we continued our flight. A plane to the right of us, however, was not so lucky. It was hit and fell burning from the sky, one of three which met such a fate during the operation. One of our men was wounded and might have been more seriously so had it not been for the protection provided by the plane's cargo and the equipment which each of us carried. "Beneš, help me take off Murphy's gear and jacket so we can check him out and stop the bleeding," I yelled.

"O.K. Sarge," Beneš answered. Feverishly he ripped off Murphy's pack and jacket and found the wound which was caused by a shell fragment. A medic stood by to help. "I guess he won't be able to make the jump. Tell the pilot he'll be staying on the plane."

The rolling and pitching caused by our pilot's evasive action continued to keep us off balance, and it was only with the greatest of difficulty that we were able to get ready for our jump when the red alert light went on. Other than Murphy, we all got off on green, but the oscillations caused a hesitation in jumping and scattered our group below. To prevent us from being falling ducks, we leaped out at heights not exceeding 800 feet. This reduced the time between leaving the plane and landing, but it also increased the risk of injury upon impact. I dropped into what seemed like a big black hole which came to life with tracers and exploding shells. I was lucky to land away from enemy fire, but two of our men injured their legs, and Pitowski, who jumped just before me, nearly drowned in the inundated fields created by the enemy's damming of the otherwise minor Douve and Merderet rivers.

While some of our units upon landing were met with devastating fire from defending German forces, Jensen, Moscowitz and I landed relatively close together between a set of hedgerows which provided us with temporary cover as we attempted to locate other members of our unit. Fortunately, what appeared to be a German patrol coming from the north turned out to be other members of our group. The crackle of small arms and machine gun fire and the sound of exploding shells could be heard from several directions, but, for the moment, none of the fire seemed to be directed at us. We saw the flames from what appeared to be a downed aircraft and a burning farmhouse. The light produced by the flames eventually revealed our positions to the Germans and the respite was short-lived. The enemy's attention had evidently been diverted away from our area by scattered airborne landings elsewhere, but now we were on the receiving end. We immediately returned the fire from our hastily-established position. Although we had an arsenal of light weapons and explosives, we were sorely in need of the heavier weapons which our glider regiments would provide when they came in. In the meantime, there ensued a fierce battle which lasted nearly half an hour. A shell landed less than 40 feet away, killing two of my buddies, Reilly and Smith, instantly, and showering me with earth. Luckily, I suffered only a small cut in the arm from this episode. The pocket of German resistance was finally silenced by a group of paratroopers attacking from the rear, but not without a number of casualties.

The first signs of dawn aided us in locating our dead and wounded. A long, grey-stone farmhouse, typical of the Normandy region, served as a temporary field hospital until we could remove the wounded to better facilities and eventually to England. The French farm family helped us by providing our men with water, food and blankets.

Several wounded German soldiers were also brought in. Two of them appeared to be no more than 17 years of age, if that. I interrogated one of them, who had the left side of his face in bandages. The medic said that the youngster would probably lose his left eye, but that he was lucky to be alive, considering the location of the wound. *"Wo kommen Sie denn her?"* I asked.

*"Aus Bayern,"* he answered.

*"Wie alt sind Sie denn?"* I continued.

*"Siebzehn,"* came his answer.

*"In welcher Kampfgruppe-sind Sie?"*

*"In der Bayerischen Einheit bei Carentan,"* he replied. (He was a 17-year old assigned to a Bavarian unit near Carentan).

But before I could go any further with the interrogation, in hopes of gaining information about the location and strength of German forces in the area, Moscowitz came running in and told me to follow him to where two of his men had found a badly wounded German soldier. I asked a medic to come with us, in case he could be of assistance. Upon reaching the spot, I thought the significance of the find was in the map and radio equipment the soldier had in his possession. But, then, I found it to be more than that. Alvarez and Jensen had been attracted by the German signalman's mutterings in English. "I am an American! Please get me a doctor! Help me! Help me!" They had been especially careful in moving towards the location of the cries in case the Germans were trying to lead them into a trap. But they found the call of distress to be genuine.

My first reaction upon reaching the wounded German soldier was one of bewilderment. It was as if I were lying there myself. A shiver ran through my body. The resemblance to my twin brother was striking; but, surely, this couldn't be he! I was not certain whether I was dreaming, having dozed off after the battle or been knocked unconscious by a German shell, or whether this was for real. Moscowitz's nudge made me mindful of the reality of the situation, and to confirm my direst suspicions, I asked the signalman for his mother's maiden name. *"Was ist der Geburtsname Ihrer Mutter?"* I asked. With great effort, he answered, "Kristina Petersen." This was enough to convince me that the wounded soldier was, indeed, the brother I had not seen for five years. I knelt down and drew him towards me, much like a father or mother would a child, tears in my eyes. Then, in a choked voice, I yelled to Alvarez to get a doctor and a stretcher, while Jensen, the medic and I tried to see what we could do in the meantime to help him. What a fate to be reunited with my brother in this way! I couldn't think of a reunion under more trying circumstances.

I was momentarily overcome by the thought of the irony and tragedy of war, which sometimes pits brother against brother, father against son, cousin against cousin, friend against friend, and, with the depersonalization of modern warfare, possibly the killing of one another without knowing it. At least in this case, there was little possibility that I was personally responsible for my brother's wounds, since they appeared to have been inflicted by shrapnel from a mortar shell or grenade, and not by a rifle bullet. But this did not·alter my bitterness over the fact that I was having to fight my own brother, and he, me. By what madness, I wondered, are nations drawn into war anyway? Is it that national leaders too often regard their subjects as mere puppets to be manipulated on the stage of history for their own personal benefit, or because modern wars are ultimately fought, not by ambitious leaders themselves, but by the innocent masses who, by accident of history, happen to be their subjects?

How absurd! Here I was, holding in my arms a member of the enemy's forces, praying for his life. Yet, at this very moment, there were Americans, British, Canadians and Frenchmen on land and at sea seeking the death or incapacitation of every German in the invasion zone, while, at the same time, German military units in the area were prepared to annihilate every Allied soldier.

Kurt did not recognize me at first because of his condition. But when I began to talk to him in German about the delicious pastries he used to make in Dad's bakery shop in Brooklyn, he looked up at me and said, *"Dann habe ich dich endlich erreicht!* (Then, I've finally reached you). He smiled as best he could and grasped at me, too weak to hug me.

But this was no time to reminisce. My brother was in danger of dying. I had perhaps already lost valuable time in trying to identify him and getting him to recognize me. We worked on him frantically. Removal of his bloodied, torn jacket revealed a deep gash in his upper right arm and a gaping wound in his right side. We stopped the flow of blood as best we could and cleansed and sterilized the wounds, administering morphine to limit what must have been excruciating pain. He was given blood plasma, and as soon as a stretcher arrived he was carried to our make-shift hospital in the farmhouse. By now the dwelling was overflowing with wounded, many of whom were screaming and moaning as they fought for life. It was a grim reminder of the horror of war!

Just as we found a place to rest the stretcher and a surgeon began to inspect Kurt's wounds, we came under a barrage of 88 millimeter shells from German guns in Carentan. The explosions were deafening. The earth shook, cracking the walls and strewing broken plaster and dust throughout the dwelling. A near miss collapsed part of the front side and tore off portions of the roof, killing several of the wounded in the kitchen. We had no choice but to lie flat on the floor. I held Kurt's hand from my position. The shelling lasted less than 10 minutes, but the dust, thundering noise, motion and falling debris it caused, coupled with the delay in attending the wounded, hastened the death of a number of the men, including my brother. Whether Kurt could have been saved in the absence of the barrage, only God knows. He was conscious when we reached the farmhouse, but not after the bombardment. The confusion caused by the attack continued to plague the ministering of care long after it was over. Kurt never regained consciousness and was dead within a half-hour. I was with him to the end of his earthly life.

Unable to help myself, I broke down and cried. What an irony that German guns should aid in Kurt's demise. On the other hand, what if he had been killed earlier by the grenade or mortar shell? Or what if he had not spoken out in English, remained silent or had been found by members of another company? I might never have experienced this reunion with him, however brief and tragic. For these few moments with him I was most grateful. I bowed my head in prayer and thanked the Lord for this gift of time and prayed that my brother would be forgiven for any injustices he might have been a party to while serving the German cause. I also prayed for an early end to this madness of death and destruction.

My communication with the Almighty helped me to recover from my remorse. But, then, I began to wonder how Kurt would have been accepted had he recovered and returned to the States. There certainly would have been little rejoicing in our Flatbush neighborhood. He probably would have had to have spent the remainder of his life in Germany, unable to face the people with whom he had grown up. He could not return home a conquering hero, as I could. In this respect, his death, however sad and however much my parents loved him, resolved a difficult problem, one that would not have to be faced once the war was over. So ended a life that had begun with so much promise!

But for now, the war was still on. For me, this longest day had a long way to go. Kurt's few personal belongings were removed and given to me. A Catholic chaplain, a paratrooper himself, administered last rites and presided over the burial of two other German and ten American soldiers who had not survived the shelling.

Among Kurt's belongings were his graduation ring from Brooklyn College and a gold band (which had been taken from his left finger), indicating that he had become engaged to an Erika Schneider on 21 February, 1943. Other than identification papers, there were pictures of Uncle Carl and cousins Christina and Margaretha from Hamburg, of Mom and Dad, of me and of Erika. There was also a recent letter from his German fiancée, in which she communicated that neither she nor any member of her family had been harmed by the air strikes of May 19 and 22 on Kiel, although a number of people had been killed. She was aware that since the escalation of the air war against German cities in 1943, the fate of relatives at home had become an increasing concern of the men on the front and in occupied territories, and reassurances such as this were as important a factor in maintaining morale as the men's own progress in battle. Ironically, the letter expressed relief that Kurt was in France and not on the eastern front. Kurt had scribbled several notes on the back of the envelope, evidently as a reminder of what he wanted to say in reply, but Allied invasion plans allowed no room for his anticipated response.

Gathering the most important of personal effects found on Kurt's person, I made a pledge to deliver this last letter and the ring to his fiancée personally after the war, if she and I were fortunate enough to survive it. A few days later, after the fall of Carentan, I, painfully, wrote a letter to Mom and Dad about my fated reunion with Kurt. I also told them of my hope to locate his fiancée after the fighting was over in order to find out more about those years in Kurt's life about which we had no knowledge. Fearful that my parents might think that I was making up this rather incredible story in order to end speculation about my brother and relieve them of any further pain, I enclosed in the letter the picture of them which Kurt had carried.

My vow to deliver the letter and engagement ring to Kurt's fiancée was not readily fulfilled. The German armies did not collapse, and the final victory was not realized by the end of the year as hoped. While the landings at the Utah beachhead were accomplished with relative ease and limited casualties, aided by our highly successful airborne operation behind enemy lines, the forces landing at Omaha Beach to the east of us were not so fortunate. In contrast to Utah, which offered a wide beach, low dunes and relatively flat terrain for our invading forces, Omaha had a narrow beach backed by high dunes and bluffs of up to 100 feet in some locations from which the German defenders could command the beach approaches. The system of underwater and beach obstacles there was one of the most extensive along the coast, and the positions were manned by crack, battle-experienced units of the Wehrmacht. From the very beginning, the operation was plagued by mishap after mishap involving landing craft and amphibious tanks, and, in the confusion, wave after wave of our troops were cut down by the savage German defense. However, the men kept coming, held the beaches, scaled the bluffs, and, through numerous acts of individual heroism, secured a small, but firm, foothold by the end of D-Day.

Still further east, along the longest stretch of beach, the British and Canadians, assisted by Free French units, experienced varying degrees of resistance, but were able to establish two secure beachheads, and the goal of landing roughly 200,000 Allied soldiers within the first 24 hours was accomplished, a feat the Germans had expected would require at least a week.

An element of surprise had been achieved by attacking in inclement weather and away from any major ports or beach resorts. The German defense was further hampered by the uncertainty as to where the landings would occur, and the 55 divisions assigned to France were widely dispersed, with only ten of them in the immediate vicinity of Normandy. Even after the landings became known, the disruption of rail and road transportation by Allied aircraft and rigidities in the German command structure impeded the rapid movement of reinforcements to the invasion points. Moreover, Field Marshal Erwin Rommel, commander of the coastal defense forces who had to return to France from a visit with his family, remained convinced for the first crucial weeks that the Normandy action was a feint and that the major assault would take place across the

Channel narrows at the Pas-de-Calais. The German divisions stationed east of the Seine were, therefore, held back until it was too late. In the meantime, the Allies continued to pour men and supplies into the expanding beachhead and to ward off all attempts to dislodge them. As the advantage turned to the Allied forces, the Germans fought tenaciously to halt the invader's advance. Caen held out for over a month, Saint Lô did not fall until July 18, and it was not until the latter part of July that the invading armies could break out of their base on the Cotentin Peninsula for their drive across France.

Having failed to stop the Allied armies at the low water mark or to destroy them away from the beaches through a concentration of power, the German army appeared doomed to defeat. Hitler was advised by members of his general staff to end the war before there was nothing left of the Reich. But their pleas fell on deaf ears. With the failure of the plot to kill Hitler July 20, 1944, hostilities were destined to continue for another nine and a half months, bringing added devastation to Germany's cities and an additional three million German casualties, as the war was fought to the bitter end. There was to be no repeat of 1918. At the time of the attempt on Hitler's life there were no foreign troops on German soil; had the conspiracy been successful and the war brought to a close, whatever the resulting territorial arrangements and penalties might have been, in the least, the German people would have been spared over half the casualties ultimately suffered in the war.

Our division returned to England in July, but in September participated in the ill-fated Nijmegen bridge jump. In December we were sent from positions in Holland to help stem the German Christmas advance through the Ardennes Forest, an incursion which became known as the Battle of the Bulge. The last months took me into the Ruhr and Bavaria. I was in Bavaria when the war ended and because of my knowledge of German was assigned to the occupation forces.

---

## * September 1945 *

Travel in Germany immediately after the war was exceedingly difficult. Mines and rubble had to be cleared. The streets through many of the large cities were all but impassable. Even getting around on foot was arduous. It was best to avoid the larger cities which had taken the brunt of the air war. There was also the problem of knowing where bridges were intact. In September, 1945 I had the opportunity to ride by jeep with two of our officers, Col. Hass and Capt. Vernon, to Bremen, where they were to meet with the British military authorities to discuss permanent use of the ports of Bremen and Bremerhaven to supply American forces in Europe. Neither could speak more than a few words of German, and I was taken along to help out in any emergency. We traveled from Frankfurt to Deutz, opposite the city of Cologne. From Deutz we could look across the Rhine to see the majestic spires of the great Cologne cathedral, still towering above the war-scarred city. The sight inspired me to write the following lines:

> "Majestic splendor, Gothic masterpiece,
> You stand amid destruction on all sides.
> Your majesty and grace were your defense
> Against the ruin which in Köln resides.
> May ne'er again such fury fierce that rents
> man's spirit, be your fortune to abide."

Upon reaching Bremen I was granted five days leave to try to locate relatives in Kiel and Hamburg. The task of finding specific individuals in the bombed-out cities was formidable. Seventy percent of Kiel had been devastated, with rubble covering sidewalks and streets and entire areas literally flattened. An address meant nothing; old street signs seldom appeared and numbers were virtually useless, as living quarters were often found in the bombed-out skeletons of buildings and in basements. Families doubled and tripled up with one another in their search for shelter. Everything was make-shift in those first few months after the war. The provision of shelter took precedent over all other reconstruction efforts. I recall going into the ruins of a bombed-out church and seeing several beautifully hewn limestone statues resting in the rubble as if on a junk pile. The struggle for survival was, at the time, more important than the resurrection of a church.

Fortunately, my mother and father had transferred to me the ability to speak German fluently. It was this very gift that had enabled Kurt to go to Berlin to study in 1939. I found that many of the residents in Kiel had been dispersed to nearby rural communities such as Eckernförde, Plön and Eutin and were no longer living in the ravaged city. In fact, Kiel's population had been reduced by nearly 40 percent as a result of the war. Through the English authorities who maintained records of registration for ration cards and a chance meeting with an elderly German woman who knew Kurt's fiancée's family, I found out that Erika Schneider and her mother were living with relatives in Melsdorf, only a few kilometers outside of Kiel. Erika's father, a high ranking naval officer, was being temporarily held by the British military authorities until he could be cleared concerning his role in the war. I walked the distance to Melsdorf in two hours, and after several inquiries located the house in which Erika and her mother were living.

This visit, as well as the one planned for Hamburg to see Uncle Carl, was as important to mother as it was to me. She was anxious to learn more about what had happened to Kurt. She was desperately looking for something which could help her purge herself of all thoughts about Kurt's being linked with the horrible Nazi regime. She wanted to find something that could renew her faith in a son who had promised so much. She constantly blamed herself for letting him go to Germany, for not preventing him from leaving on this "journey into darkness," merely to fulfill a dream she had had since the two of us were small children. She had suffered so much grief, not just from the loss of a child, but from a child who had destroyed the image she had of him. I was hoping that I would find something which could help explain what happened. Mom was not convinced that it was just love for a girl that kept Kurt from returning home.

A surprising, but certainly not unnatural, thing happened when I went to the door. A young woman who appeared to be in her early twenties answered my knock. When she saw me, she threw her arms around me, kissed me and began to cry, saying *"Ich wusste, du würdest zurück kommen"* (I knew you would return). I held her, but could not at first reply in kind. Kurt and I were almost identical in appearance. Perhaps my face was somewhat fuller, but someone who didn't know us well could hardly tell us apart. I assumed immediately that the young woman was Kurt's fiancée, and that she thought he had survived the war. She could not understand my seeming lack of emotion, although I continued to hold her, stroking her brownish blond hair. I then pulled myself back and explained to her that I was not Kurt, but his twin brother, Carl. *"Leider, bin ich nicht Kurt, sondern sein Bruder Carl."*

Kurt, I explained, had been killed in France; I was here to deliver to her the last letter she had sent to him, the envelope with his scribbled notes and his engagement ring. She was overwhelmed by the news of Kurt's death, clutching me and crying in grief. I was moved by the intensity of her feelings and also broke down and cried. In trying to console her, I was pulled by a strong attraction, as if she belonged to me. Our mutual grief at once drew us together and helped to relieve the tension of the moment. I became so ecstatic I did not want to stop holding her. But her mother's appearance ended that, and we were asked to come to the front room to drink some peppermint tea which she had prepared.

Mrs. Schneider invited me to visit her and Erika as often as I wished, perhaps seeing in me a means of providing emotional support for her daughter, as well as having someone on the side of the victorious powers who could be helpful during this difficult period.

The next two days were filled with storytelling. I explained how I had found Kurt during the early hours of the Normandy invasion and had stayed with him until his death. Erika, in turn, gave an account which extended over four years, from the time she had met Kurt at Bad Salzuflen during the summer of 1940 to his last letter in May, 1944. She related how Kurt had come to join the Wehrmacht and why he happened to be in France at the time of the invasion. By 1943 Kurt, having recovered from wounds he received while with German forces near Stalingrad the previous year, openly announced to her his disenchantment over his decision to enter the German army. Following his recuperation, he succeeded, with the intervention of her father, in being transferred to France. He had no intention of fighting the Allied armies which, he felt, would eventually be landing there, unless

Germany collapsed from the onslaught of the Red Army beforehand. His goal, according to Erika, was to surrender to the first Allied units he came into contact with. In other words, he had sought a transfer to France to be away from the eastern front and to provide the opportunity for giving himself up to the Allies. Erika had said nothing about this to her father, who thought that, while the Russian front was fraught with unpredictabilities, the French theater could remain quiet for years. He had developed a strong liking for the young American and utilized his contacts in Berlin to make the transfer possible.

When no letters arrived after June 6, 1944, Erika had thought that Kurt's plan had succeeded, that he had been captured by American or British forces which would be anxious to use the information he had about German military units in France. She was not disturbed by the missing-in-action communication that she had received from German authorities, since, she felt, he would naturally be missing-in-action if he had been captured by Allied forces. It was no wonder that Erika had anticipated Kurt's return and that my American uniform had seemingly confirmed that event.

I had so much to tell Mom and Dad, but I still wanted to visit Uncle Carl, after whom I was named, in Blankenese in the two days remaining before I had to return to Bremen. Before leaving, however, I promised Erika and her mother that I would try to return before the end of the year. There were restrictions on fraternization with Germans, but the Schneiders were, to me, relatives who needed help. My promise to return was genuine, for I had taken a strong initial liking to the young woman whom my brother had left behind. I guess I was charmed by the same traits that had attracted him.

Although Blankenese was not spared by the bombings, it was far enough up the Elbe River from the center of Hamburg not to have experienced the full fury of the fire storm which had engulfed the core area after repeated bombings between July 25 and August 2, 1943. The greatest damage was caused by a single block buster in March, 1943 which destroyed seven dwellings and caused widespread damage. Uncle Carl's bakery had received only minor damage from concussion and flying debris. When I first met him, he was clothed in a white undershirt and white apron, having come directly from the bakery where he was preparing dough for next morning's baking. He wore glasses and his hairline was receding and graying. I had written that I would be coming and was recognized immediately. My resemblance to Kurt became the first topic of conversation. Shortly thereafter, Tante Elsa and cousin Margaretha made their appearance. I held them and asked how everything was going. They immediately related how fortunate they had been in comparison with so many people in Hamburg, where 55,000 people had been killed by the bombings, about 42,000 alone during the series of massive raids in July/August, 1943. There were damaged and destroyed buildings and homes in Blankenese, but not the total devastation that characterized vast sections of the Hamburg city center, particularly the eastern portions and Wandsbek.

I repeated my story about being reunited with Kurt in the early hours of the Normandy invasion. Uncle Carl and Aunt Elsa had been informed that Kurt was missing-in-action and presumed dead and had told Erika, but they were not aware of Kurt's plan to surrender to Allied units. Erika had kept that to herself for fear of endangering Kurt's life.

Because they were fortunate enough to have a house that survived the war, my uncle and aunt had to share it with five other people. One bedroom was given over to an elderly couple who had lost their apartment in Altona in 1943. The family room became the home of a widow, who had lost her husband on the Russian front, and her two children, a boy and a girl. The widow had fled Berlin in late March, just prior to the Russian assault on the city. A single kitchen and two bathrooms (a full bath upstairs and a half bath downstairs) had to be shared by three families comprised of eight people. But Uncle Carl said they felt lucky, for one family they knew on the Auguste-Baurstrasse had 16 persons in their home. Every room, including the basement, was being used for housing, even though the house had suffered sizable damage.

This was their long introduction for excusing their inability to provide me with a separate bedroom, as they had for Kurt on his first visit in 1939, but I found the veranda sofa quite satisfactory. After all, I had become accustomed to sleeping in uncomfortable places, including on the ground during my combat days.

For the next two days I listened attentively to my uncle's and aunt's recollections of Kurt, how he had spent his first weeks with them and how he visited them on different occasions, including the last, just after Christmas in 1943. They had a number of letters from him, from Berlin, the Russian front, the military hospital in Germany and from France. Since they had no sons, only two daughters, they had looked upon Kurt as an adopted son. He was thought of as their contribution to the German military effort. In contrast, Mom and Dad were aware of Kurt's activities only up to August 1941, about the time he joined the German army. Whether he tried to write us after that, we don't know; no letters were received. But he did continue to write his aunt and uncle and fiancée-to-be in Germany.

These letters were very helpful in piecing together that period of Kurt's life that we knew nothing about, and they assisted me in trying to explain to my parents what had transpired in Germany after August, 1941. Uncle Carl gave me several pictures showing Kurt in his Wehrmacht uniform. He also showed pictures from the Christmases and New Years Kurt spent in Blankenese while a student in Berlin. Our discussions of how Kurt came to join the German cause were most intriguing; they spurred my own desire to learn more about the events leading up to the Second World War and the dynamics of totalitarian movements.

Before my return to Bremen, Uncle Carl wanted me to meet Erna Dietz, an elderly neighbor whom Kurt had saved after her house had been hit during one of the seven air attacks on Hamburg in July/August, 1943. She had been pinned in the wreckage of her home. Kurt, assisting the clean-up forces, had heard her weak cries, and, with the help of a warden, had extricated her. She had evidently been knocked temporarily unconscious, so the civil defense units had not been immediately aware of her presence in the rubble. Fortunately, there had been no fire. A piece of broken timber from the roof supports had ripped a huge gash in her leg, causing considerable bleeding. Because of her condition, it was necessary for her to have a blood transfusion immediately. Kurt had volunteered his blood. Frau Dietz attributed her survival to Kurt's action. When she met me, she hugged me and said, "Bless you!" On this occasion she gave me a letter addressed to mother, mentioning how thankful she was to Kurt for saving her life. I sent this letter, along with a lengthy account of my two visits, to mother, and it became a source of great relief to her. Kurt's joining the Wehrmacht and fighting the Russians could be explained while the United States was still neutral, but not after the United States had entered the war. Many Americans had joined the Lincoln Brigade during the Spanish Civil War to fight Fascism. Wasn't this the same, only reversed? But after December 11, 1941, when Germany declared war on the United States, the fact could not be explained away.

The letter from Frau Dietz helped to restore mother's faith in her lost son. He could still be thought of as a good boy, but one who had been misguided.

I had to return to Bremen to catch my ride back to Frankfurt. In spite of the distance between Frankfurt and the two north German cities, I made the trip a number of times before returning to the United States in 1948. None of these later trips was as difficult as the first. Mom and Dad sent food parcels and clothing to Uncle Carl and the Schneiders during much of this time, as postal rates were reduced to only a few cents a pound to facilitate such help during a very difficult period. My trips to Kiel were to become more than just visits as time went on, always under the guise of visiting relatives, and Erika and I were given permission to marry in August, 1948.

Upon my return to Brooklyn with my new bride, I worked with Dad in the family bakery, but after a short time decided to go to college under the G.I. Bill to try to start where my brother had left off nearly a decade earlier. It was at Queens College that I was able to learn more about the appeal of totalitarianism. The Nuremberg War Crime trials had just been concluded and books such as Erich Fromm's *Escape From Freedom* were available for study. It was during this period that I decided to use the information at my disposal to write this story about Kurt.

# CHAPTER II

# An Uncertain Journey

Kurt and I were born about 30 minutes apart in the Brooklyn home of our parents in 1917, just four days prior to the entrance of the United States into "the war to end all wars." Mom and Dad had come to this country from Hamburg, Germany, in 1910 shortly after their marriage. Dad had learned the trade of a baker and readily found work as a helper in a small neighborhood bakery in Brooklyn. By working long hours, he was able to save enough money to set up a small bake shop of his own in 1916.

Despite the unpopularity of the use of German both during and immediately after the war, our parents, at least at home, spoke German to us from the day we were born, so as we grew up Kurt and I became as fluent in German as in English. Fortunately, because of the two of us (at least that is what we were told), Dad never had to serve in the war.

It was my mother's dream to be able to send one or both of us to study in Germany when we were old enough. This dream seems to have been nurtured by the fact that, as a child, she, though quite bright, was unable to go beyond the *mittlere Reife* (equivalent of eleven years of schooling) because of her parents' economic status. The dream remained unshaken even by the hardship of the Depression and the rise to power of Adolf Hitler in Germany. The Depression had been hard on us, because many of our neighbors were not always able to pay us for the bread and other baked goods that they sought. However, they tried to make up for it in other ways by helping with the plumbing, repairing and cleaning the ovens, painting, or giving us things. On Saturday evenings we gladly distributed leftover baked goods to families most in need.

At least Dad had work, and he had customers. Mother worked at the counter, and both Kurt and I helped out after school and on Saturdays when we were old enough. By the time we graduated from high school in 1935, mother had saved enough money to allow Kurt to attend college. But Kurt continued to put in 20 hours a week at the bakery to help with the costs. He became quite a good baker himself and probably would have made a success of it, but that wasn't what mother was sending him to college for. Because he lived at home, the expenses of attending the Brooklyn College Branch of the City College system were minimal. When the College moved to its new campus on Bedford Avenue in 1937, Kurt was able to walk to school. He graduated in 1939.

For some reason, I was not the student that Kurt was. We had graduated together from high school, but I had neither the grades nor the desire then to go on to college. Besides, Dad needed help in the bakery and I enjoyed making everything from bear claws to wedding cakes. I can't say that I was duller, but serious books at the time were just not my cup of tea. Kurt, on the other hand, spent most of his leisure hours reading both fictional and non-fictional works. As a history major, with an emphasis on modern Europe, he read extensively about the origins and consequences of the 1914-18 World War. Novels about the war, including Hemingway's *Farewell to Arms* and Remarque's *All Quiet on the Western Front,* were also in his collection. Kurt dated occasionally, but never developed a serious relationship with any of his female acquaintances. He enjoyed swimming and running, and, while in high school, gained recognition in the crawl and 100 and 200 yard dashes. Because of his accomplishments and out-going personality, Kurt seemed to be well-liked by both his classmates and teachers. He always had more friends than I had.

The question of studying in Germany became problematical with each new controversial move of Adolf Hitler. The German dictator had been viewed initially as a nationalist, interested merely in bringing the German people together again and creating some kind of order out of chaos, even if it meant eliminating certain opponents and creating a police state. As young as I was, I had certain apprehensions about the German up-start, but Kurt became quite fascinated with him. Although Mom and Dad told Kurt to keep his thoughts about Hitler to himself, out of concern for what neighbors and customers might think, there was no question from his conversations with me that during his undergraduate years at Brooklyn College, Kurt was strongly supportive of the German dictator's actions. While I cannot say exactly what shaped his thoughts, he certainly was not influenced at home. Mom and Dad were very low key politically and were as concerned as I was over events in Germany. Kurt's extensive readings may have nourished certain attitudes and feelings about the German cause. In any case, he felt strongly that it was Hitler who could return Germany to its rightful place in the world of nations, not as a weakling, but as a power that other countries, especially France, would respect.

I don't think Kurt ever considered where all this would lead. He viewed the remilitarization of the Rhineland in 1936 and, later on, the *Anschluss* (union) with Austria as legitimate and justifiable acts. "After all," he would say, "didn't Germany have a sovereign right to place its armed forces any place on its own soil?" On the other hand, "Weren't the interests of an emaciated Austria best served in union with Germany?" I had to admit that there was much support for Kurt's conclusions.

But the summer of 1938 was a different story. Germany began to make threatening gestures against Czechoslovakia, and war appeared imminent. Kurt had finished his junior year in college and events in Europe could alter his plans to study in Germany after graduation. Arrangements had to be made prior to the end of the year. Kurt always claimed that Hitler did not want war, but merely wanted to get back what was rightfully Germany's. Kurt also didn't think the British and French would fight. "After all," he exclaimed, "why would Britain and France go to war over the Sudetenland or the Corridor? They are not British or French possessions, and any boundary modifications do not threaten either power."

Mom asked Kurt to make other plans, perhaps to go to Columbia or NYU for graduate study. Kurt wanted to wait, however, for he just couldn't contemplate a war occurring over Czechoslovakia. Events in late September almost proved him wrong, as Hitler threatened war if he did not have the Sudetenland by October 1, 1938. The world held its breath, ultimately to be given an eleven-month reprieve by the infamous Munich Agreement, an arrangement which appeared to give Hitler all he wanted.

For our family, the Munich Agreement was crucial, for it cleared the major obstacle to making a final decision about Kurt's studies the following year. Kurt obtained an application for an American passport and sought visa information from the German General Consulate in New York. For information on studying in Germany he visited the German University Service office, which had been opened in New York under considerable opposition from various quarters because of the German government's domestic policies. (Within a half-year the branch was closed on request of the U.S. State Department on grounds of actual or alleged espionage activities.)

For Kurt, it was now "Peace for our time." Hitler had what he wanted. However, I felt that Danzig and the Polish Corridor, which separated East Prussia from the rest of Germany, could still cause a problem later. The failure of Britain and France to act in March, 1939, over the final absorption of Czechoslovakia into the Reich tended to support Kurt's contention that there would be no war, that as long as there was no "direct" threat to Britain and France, they would not intervene.

The realization of Mom's dream of having a child study in Germany was tempered by the possible outbreak of a war which might prevent her son's return to America. But, with the crisis seemingly over, Kurt was booked on the July 24, 1939 sailing of the Bremen, a month after his graduation.

Kurt chose the Friedrich Wilhelm University in Berlin over Hamburg or Kiel because, as a modern history major, he wanted to be at the seat of political activity in Germany. He also wanted to see Hitler personally, hoping, thereby, to gain a better understanding of the leader's hold on the German people. Kurt was fascinated by the dynamism of the National Socialist movement and by its ability to accomplish so much in only a few short years. Not even Roosevelt, Kurt would argue, had been able to put our country back to work, and Roosevelt and Hitler came to power in 1933 only a few weeks apart. The ruthlessness of Hitler's movement seemed not to disturb him.

Mom would rather have had Kurt study in Hamburg or Kiel. In either city he would have been away from the influence of that "Austrian Madman," as Mom called the German leader. Moreover, Uncle Carl, father's brother after whom I was named, lived just outside Hamburg, and there were several distant relatives in Kiel. Mom was very much worried about her son's welfare, even though he was now 22 and had developed a strong mind of his own. She had lost a brother and two cousins on the German side in the Great War of 1914-18 and did not want to lose a son in any future war.

I can remember those last few weeks before Kurt's sailing as if it were yesterday. Not only was there his festive graduation, but we twice visited the New York World's Fair, in which 60 nations participated. Dr. Edward Beneš, former President of Czechoslovakia and victim of the Munich Agreement, dedicated the Czecho-Slovak Pavilion at the Fair, even though his country no longer existed as an independent entity, having been absorbed into Hitler's Reich a few months earlier. Germany did not participate in the event, whose theme was "The World of Tomorrow." King George VI and Queen Elizabeth of Great Britain were visitors in early June; they met with President Roosevelt who, after the fall of Czechoslovakia, was anxious to strengthen Anglo-American relations.

Twice I accompanied Kurt to Manhattan to help him complete his wardrobe. He found one suit he liked for $15.00, but then splurged on a nice pin-stripe for $25.00. He also bought presents for Uncle Carl's family, as he would be staying with them for several weeks before completing a short tour of Germany and going on to Berlin, and he wanted to take along a few Christmas gifts which might not be available on the Continent.

At times the excitement made me wish I were going along. But the news coming out of Europe was enough to make anyone hesitant. From Czechoslovakia Hitler had turned to Danzig and the Corridor, in spite of an announcement by Prime Minister Neville Chamberlain that Britain would aid Poland in the event of an attack. There was growing opinion that Britain really meant it this time. Yet, there continued to be a lingering feeling that she would back down in a crisis situation as she had done before. At least Hitler acted as if he expected a British retreat; after all, why should Britain go to war over a city (Danzig) that was 95 percent German? The situation would have seemed to dictate more restraint had Hitler really anticipated British and French intervention.

The increasing tension was not to Mom's liking, and as late as two days before the scheduled sailing she tried to get Kurt to change his mind. Kurt had a way of soothing Mom. "Ah, Mom, Hitler's too smart to get into war over Danzig. Poland will not agree to German occupation of Danzig simply because Hitler wants it. He has to create enough uncertainty to force Poland and Britain to back down. Didn't we resort to bluff and bravado in 1846 over the Oregon question and on several occasions in the Caribbean to get our way? Why not Germany?"

It all sounded so logical and put Mom at ease. Dad brought down from the attic an old sea trunk in which he and Mom had brought their belongings from Germany nearly thirty years before. We had some good laughs over the idea of this somewhat bruised box affair's (dubbed *Mottenkiste* 'moth box' by Mom and Dad) returning to its land of origin. It was packed with books and clothing and sent to the pier as hold-luggage the evening before the sailing.

I remember waving to Kurt that evening as the Bremen pulled away from the 46th Street pier into the Hudson River for one of its last voyages to Germany. (Just a month later, the Bremen, to avoid internment in New York, evaded the British blockade with a high-speed dash across the Atlantic to Murmansk in the Soviet Union, arriving there September 6, 1939.) It was the last time I was to see him until that fateful day in Normandy five years later. He left us with all the energy and aspirations of youth, oblivious to the fate that awaited him. We had expected to meet him again the following summer when I was to accompany Mom and Dad to Hamburg to celebrate the thirtieth anniversary of their emigration to America.

There were other ships that Kurt could have taken to Germany, including the Washington of the United States Lines and the Hamburg of the Hamburg-American Line, but the North German Lloyd's Bremen, with accommodations for 2,000 passengers, was particularly popular with American tourists and Kurt wanted to take it. On her maiden voyage in July, 1929 she won the legendary blue riband from the Cunard's Mauretania with an average speed of 27.83 knots and remained one of the fastest ships on the North Atlantic run for the next decade.

It was nearly a month before we received our first letter from Kurt. We were just as anxious to hear about the relatives as about Kurt's impressions of Germany. His letter, as translated from the German, read as follows:

August 4, 1939
Hamburg-Blankenese

Dear Mom, Dad and Carl,

I'm writing this letter from my bedroom in Blankenese after having returned from an unforgettable tour of Hamburg. The trip across the Atlantic was really exciting. Not only is the Bremen an elegant ship, but the meals and service were superb. We could often select from up to ten different dishes from an elaborate menu. For example, the last night on board we had potted goose-liver on butter toast, salad Monte Christo, turtle soup, grilled salmon, roast beef, preserved plums, peas and carrots, cauliflower, hazelnut cream, Cheshire pie, and an assortment of cheeses and fruits. I'll send a menu in my next letter.

There was dancing and swimming and many interesting people to talk to. As you can well imagine, much of the conversation revolved around speculation about war. There was great concern, but, at least among those I talked to, including Germans, the consensus was that there would be no war either because the British and French would make whatever concessions were necessary to avoid it, or Hitler would be careful not to push things so far as to make war inevitable, since Germany was not now ready for a major conflict. But, it is not the purpose of this letter to upset you over war talk.

Uncle Carl and Aunt Elsa met the ship in Bremerhaven, and we traveled to Hamburg by train and from there by S-Bahn to Blankenese. Uncle Carl said that if I had come one year later, he would have picked me up in a car. He was making weekly installments on a new people's car (*Volkswagen*) which was to be mass-produced for less than 1,000 marks. He showed me a detailed prospectus. I must admit, it looked more like a lady bug than a car. Certainly, nothing like the big American automobiles. But they are probably more appropriate for the narrow German roads. Hitler has been building some high-speed motor roads, but they presently connect only a few cities.

Uncle Carl's bakery shop is somewhat smaller than ours, but business is good. Uncle Carl and Aunt Elsa tried to avoid any discussion about Hitler, except to say that he had brought order to the country and that they had personally benefited from the improvement in the economy since 1933, when the National Socialists came to power. Uncle Carl spoke of the terrible riot that had occurred in Altona (then a suburb of

Hamburg) on July 17, 1932, between Nazis and Communists. Before it was quelled, 18 people were killed and 285 wounded. It occurred when a group of Nazis under police escort were shot at while parading through a predominantly working-class area of the city, he said. It scared many of us, being so close. Such things don't occur anymore, he assured me. Although trying to remain apolitical, he was concerned that Hitler's policies might lead to war. He had been on the West Front during the Great War and had no desire to see a repetition of it. I tried not to press the conversation, since it was obvious that they were uneasy discussing it.

Margaretha was out of school and helped in the bakery while Christina was completing her *mittlere Reife*. But the most interesting part of the visit was seeing pictures of grandmother and grandfather Schröder and their parents. I also saw pictures of Mom's brother who was killed in 1916 on the Western front and of Uncle Carl in his uniform from the Great War.

Blankenese is certainly a lovely place. We walked along the heights overlooking the Elbe River, and down through the woods to the esplanade along the river bank. It was a steep walk up the house-lined narrow streets to the heights above where the major part of the town lies. Blankenese contains many splendid villas. Uncle Carl's home, however, is a smaller three-bedroom, red-brick dwelling about the size of our home.

I'll try to write every few weeks. Before going to Berlin, I plan to visit Bremen, Cologne, Frankfurt, Heidelberg, Munich and Dresden. Don't worry about me, and don't worry about war. There won't be any!

With all my love, Kurt

Kurt found prewar Hamburg a city of striking beauty and immediately became captivated by it. He even considered favoring Hamburg over Berlin for his studies, but in the end stayed with Berlin because of its political importance. He described Hamburg to me in one of his letters, contributing considerable historical information.

August 11, 1939
Hamburg-Blankenese

Dear Carl,

I promised to write you and share with you some of my impressions of Hamburg. Rarely has nature blessed a city with such scenic diversity, and I know you'll like Hamburg when you come to Germany with Mom and Dad next summer. Situated on the Elbe River 70 miles (110 kilometers) inland from the North Sea, it emerged as an important seaport in the 12th century when Emperor Frederick I Barbarossa granted it free navigation of the Elbe with the right to levy duties on foreign shipping. In 1241 it joined in the formation of the Hanseatic League, an association of North German trading cities.

Its early settlers dammed the Alster River, a small tributary of the Elbe, to form a large and a small lake (known as the Aussenalster and Binnenalster around which the city grew. The Aussenalster is particularly good for sailing. The avenues bordering the Binnenalster are among the most fashionable streets in the city, carrying such names as Jungfernstieg and Ballindamm (formerly Alsterdamm), named after the developer of the Hamburg-America Line, Albert Ballin.

A vast network of canals, harbors, dock installations and shipbuilding yards was constructed on the Alster and the numerous islands between the northern and southern branches of the Elbe River to handle and build all sizes of ships. The skyline of the city is dominated by the city hall, built in German Renaissance style near the turn of the century, and five large church towers, the tallest of which, St. Nicholas (*Nikolai-Kirche*), rises 483 feet above street level, making it the third highest religious edifice in the world. The Nikolai church was built as a memorial to the fire of 1842 which destroyed one-fourth of the city center. With the removal of the ramparts and fortifications around the older part of the city in the 19th century, large areas were opened up for public gardens and tree-lined promenades. In Hagenbeck, the city possesses one of the finest zoological gardens in the world. We'll be sure to see it on your visit next year.

I'm fine and having a great time. I'll write you again from Berlin. Tell Mom and Dad not to worry about me.

Your brother, Kurt

In 1939 Hamburg was Germany's largest seaport and an important supplier of naval vessels and combat aircraft for Hitler's military machine. The giant battleship Bismarck had been launched in February 1939 from the city's Blohm and Voss shipyards and was being outfitted there. The launching had been a state occasion, with Hitler, Admiral Raeder, Göring, Goebbels, Hess, and Himmler among the spectators. Dorothea von Löwenfelt, Otto von Bismarck's granddaughter, christened the ship to the cheers of a huge crowd and blaring bands. Uncle Carl and Aunt Elsa had watched the spectacle as best they could from Landungsbrücken on the Elbe River bank.

Hamburg's population had been swelled to 1,700,000 in 1937 by the realignment of boundaries which consolidated Hamburg with Altona, Wandsbek and Harburg-Wilhelmsburg (which had belonged to Prussia) in exchange for Cuxhaven, at the mouth of the Elbe, expanding the size of the city from 160 to 291 square miles.

Kurt was to return to Hamburg on a number of occasions during the next several years, the last times just before the massive bombing attacks during the summer of 1943, and again just after Christmas 1943.

Kurt sent another lengthy letter to us, along with the promised menu, just prior to his tour of Germany. He also sent several postcards along the way, noting the beauty of the Rhine and the distinctive character of the individual cities he visited. But he was anxious to get to Berlin to fmd a room and get firmly settled prior to the beginning of classes in the fall.

During the months of July and August tensions over Poland increased. While the Western newspapers stressed Germany's menacing position, the German news media played up the Polish threat to Danzig and to the peace of Europe. The mood among most Germans was that this would not come to war, that Hitler would somehow resolve the crisis over Danzig without war, just as he had resolved other crises.

Kurt arrived in Berlin from Dresden on August 22 and immediately began looking for a room. The Humboldt Haus at the University gave him the names of several families that specifically sought out students. Kurt had some definite ideas about where he wanted to live. For one, he didn't want to be too far from the University and the Wilhelmstrasse, nor did he want to be too far from the pulse of life in the city. He ended up selecting a room in Charlottenburg just off the Wilmersdorfer Strasse, near a small church. Besides being close to public transportation on the Kant Strasse, he was within walking distance of the zoological gardens, Kurfürsten-Damm, and the Charlottenburger Chaussee, the route of most parades. Once he had an address, he registered with the Berlin authorities as required by law.

Kurt's room was rather large. He had use of the kitchen to warm things up, and his arrangement included supper with Herr and Frau Schulz. Kurt had the room in the apartment which had been occupied formerly by the Schulzes' two daughters, both of whom were now married. Kurt picked up milk, rolls, fruit and other items at a series of small stores along the Wilmersdorfer Strasse. He usually purchased only a half liter of milk each day, ladled into a small bucket. The Schulz family was able to supplement its income with the 30 additional marks that they received from Kurt each month. Initially, Kurt ate his major meals at the University.

Kurt spent his first several days in Berlin exploring the vastness of the German capital. With the unification of the city and its suburbs in 1920, Berlin became a municipality extending over 341 square miles. In spite of the relative flatness of the landscape, Kurt found Berlin a city of great natural beauty, with almost one-half of its territory consisting of parks, forests and water areas. The Spree River, which flows through the center of Berlin, comes together with the Havel near the city's western boundaries to form a series of lakes, including Grosser Wannsee and Tegeler See, and other waterways for such pleasantries as rowing, sailing and swimming. The beaches at Wannsee near Potsdam reminded Kurt of Coney Island on a weekend. Grünewald, on the western reaches of the City, was, with its 7,400 acres (11.5 square miles), nearly as large as some medium-size cities, and the Tiergarten, only slightly smaller than New York City's Central Park, provided both a park and a zoo right in the center of the city. The medieval appearance which characterized portions of Hamburg was lacking in Berlin, the latter having witnessed most of its development after the end of the Napoleonic Wars. Under the guidance of a series of far-sighted Prussian monarchs, the city was marked by a distinct spaciousness. Kurt was struck by the wide boulevards, the public squares, the large public buildings, monuments and museums. Unter den Linden, Berlin's most famous street, was nearly 200 feet wide, including the center park-like strip which separated the two directions of traffic. There were only a few tall buildings in the city, such as the Karstadt department store building in South Berlin and Columbus Haus on Potsdamer Platz, but none exceeded 13 stories. This was in stark contrast to the Manhattan skyline that Kurt knew so well, but, however different, it did not take Kurt long to fall in love with Berlin.

Like Hamburg, Berlin was served by an elaborate public transportation network of subways, interurban trains, street cars and buses (Berlin had some 600 double-deckers), making all parts of the city easily accessible within a matter of minutes. Bicycles were also widely used, as were horse-drawn taxis.

Until 1871 Germany was a nation without a true capital. With unification and the consolidation of governmental activities in Berlin, the city grew rapidly from 800,000 to a bustling metropolis of nearly four and a half million in 1939. Assisted by the 1920 consolidation it became the largest city in continental Europe and the fourth largest in the world after London, New York and Tokyo. In 1937 Adolf Hitler began a vast building program, including public structures and upgrading of the Berlin transportation system. The project was still in progress when Kurt came to the German capital.

Kurt had arrived in Berlin just one day prior to the signing of the German-Soviet non-aggression pact, which ultimately cleared the way for the invasion of Poland. Berliners with whom Kurt spoke were happy at the outcome, since it eliminated the possibility of Germany having to fight a two-front war, a traditional fear of the German people. Many felt that Britain and France, without Russian support, would not now risk a move. Nevertheless, Kurt noticed anti-aircraft weapons being positioned in various parts of the city, and on August 27 rationing was instituted for certain food items, soap, coal, shoes and textiles. A clothing card based on points was also distributed. The institution of rationing cards, coupled with the cancellation of the Nazi party rally at Nuremberg and seeming lack of progress on the diplomatic front, created an uneasiness not known earlier among Berliners. Kurt paid close attention to what people on street cars and on the street were saying about the situation and sensed little enthusiasm for a war which seemed avoidable. The Poles had ordered general mobilization, but few considered Poland to be a serious threat. Berliners appeared more concerned with whatever actions Britain and France might take if hostilities were to break out. But their fate was not for them to decide.

They could only wait and hope that their Führer would do everything in his power to avoid war. For now they were being told nothing, and whatever optimism there had been earlier in the week had faded by nightfall of August 31, 1939.

Berliners woke up the next morning to learn that their country was at war. In the early hours of September 1, 1939, units of the Wehrmacht had marched into Poland in lightning-like fashion, crushing all resistance in their path. Two days later, after Hitler refused to honor a British-French ultimatum to withdraw German forces from Poland, the world erupted into war. It appears that Hitler was convinced all the while that the British would not fight over Poland. His Chief of the Wehrmacht high command, General Wilhelm Keitel, had assured him a German-Soviet partition of Poland would be accepted as *fait accompli*. But this time the British held firm, seeing that appeasement would never satisfy the German leader. The general enthusiasm that marked Germany's entrance into the Great War in 1914 was strikingly absent in 1939. Rather, most Berliners were stunned, unbelieving that their Führer had drawn them into a world conflict over the problem of the Corridor.

Mother was frantic over the events in Europe. She telephoned the State Department in Washington to find out what could be done. She was informed that the American Embassy in Berlin had issued a communication on August 26 requesting all Americans in Germany whose presence was "not absolutely necessary" to leave the country.

Although the United States was not itself at war, she was told to inform her son that he should leave Germany immediately if he had not already done so. It was still possible to return to the United States through Scandinavia, the Netherlands, Italy, Greece or Portugal. The Trans-Siberian railroad was also an outside possibility, she was told.

Mother then called the German Embassy repeatedly, but failed to get through for several days. When she finally made contact, she was assured that Kurt was perfectly safe in Berlin. There was no fighting on German soil. Germany did not want war with Britain and France and was working for an amicable settlement. Although he did not state so directly, the embassy spokesman left mother with the impression that the war would not last long, that some kind of an agreement would ultimately be negotiated. The events of the next several months seemed to substantiate this impression. No British and French forces were sent to Poland. There was no German invasion of France nor a Franco-British move against Germany, and the air war was limited to a few nuisance raids against naval targets in Cuxhaven and Wilhelmshaven. Both sides took great care to avoid missions that would endanger civilian populations.

Poland was eliminated as an independent state within three weeks, although Warsaw held out until September 27th, the victim of what came to be known as *Blitzkrieg* (lightning war).

Nevertheless, mother sent a wire to Kurt in care of the American Embassy in Berlin, where he was picking up his mail until he established a permanent address, asking him to return home on the first available ship and to postpone his studies in Germany until a more favorable time.

The inability to communicate directly with her son was both frustrating and worrisome for mother.

The cards that we were receiving from Kurt had been written during his trip to southern Germany, prior to the outbreak of war. His first letter from Berlin did not arrive until September 20th even though he had mailed it August 25th. In it he expressed the opinion, which proved to be incorrect, that the German-Soviet accord had removed the possibility of war in the near future by making Britain and France more reluctant to take action.

Not until the first week of October did we receive a letter from Kurt indicating that he had received the warning from the American Embassy and mother's telegram. His feeling was that the war would be over within a few months. While there were blackouts and air raid alerts, no bombs had fallen on Berlin or any other German city. He was determined to stick it out. As it turned out, Kurt matriculated for the fall semester and went on with his studies as if there were no war at all. In fact, after the fall of Poland there was no war, except at sea. Germans refrained from bombing Britain out of fear of angering the British public and undermining peace efforts, and the British restricted their sorties to photo reconnaissance, the dropping of propaganda leaflets and attacks on naval ships. Except for clashes between small patrols, the Western front was characterized by a bewildering inactivity, as the contenders sat behind their seemingly impregnable fortifications, confident of their ability to repel any attack. This period came to be known as the Phoney War or *Sitzkrieg* (sitting war). It came to a sudden end on April 9, 1940, with the German invasion of Denmark and Norway and the invasion of the Low Countries and France a month later.

# CHAPTER III
# The Transformation

Initially it appeared that Kurt's decision to remain in Germany had been the right one. In the months immediately following the fall of Poland there was a general lack of conflict, and Berliners, including Kurt, went about their business much as in peace time. All along, Kurt felt that some resolution of differences between the contending sides would be found and that the existing situation would not deteriorate into an all-out struggle; otherwise he would have returned home.

Rumors of a possible settlement were rampant during the last week of September and first part of October in that first year of war. Germany indicated that it had no claims in the West and was willing to conclude peace if England and France recognized the existing partition of Poland; but the initiative was rejected by the two allies. Even as late as July, 1940, after the fall of France, Hitler made a peace overture, and had there existed a government in Berlin that the British felt they could trust and which was willing to withdraw from the occupied countries, subject to some revision of boundaries, Europe might have been spared the horror which was eventually to engulf it. But any peace under Hitler would have condemned the occupied peoples of Europe to virtual slavery and destroyed whatever hope they might have had of becoming free again, as well as posing an intolerable threat to Britain on the European Continent. The German dictator had, time after time, demonstrated the worthlessness of his promises, and the Churchill government (in July 1940) chose to continue the war rather than risk a one-sided and uncertain peace which could be terminated at any time at Hitler's will.

Although Americans almost universally abhorred the Hitler regime and hoped for a British victory, there was little support for direct American involvement in the conflict. The German government, anxious to keep the United States out of the European fracas, sought to cultivate this noninterventionist sentiment, while the British waged a competing propaganda effort for American support. Charles Lindbergh, the popular American aviator who had been a close observer of the German military build-up, became an early opponent of intervention, rejecting the argument that the best way to defend America was to defend Britain. Fearing the growing power of Japan and the Soviet Union, Lindbergh warned of the threat to western civilization of a protracted conflict which left Britain and Germany prostrate and supported a quick negotiated settlement. His remarks were widely quoted in the German press. Others supported a settlement, feeling that this would free Hitler to destroy an even greater menace, the Soviet Union. A Europe dominated by Germany would be preferable to one dominated by the Soviet Union. But would a victorious Germany have stopped there? Still others, among them isolationist senators William Borah (Idaho), Gerald Nye (North Dakota) and Burton K. Wheeler (Montana), radio commentator Gerald L. K. Smith, the Hearst newspapers, pacifists and Communists, opposed American involvement in Europe's quarrels for a variety of reasons.

Meanwhile, in Germany, American reporters were given double rations, favorable exchange rates and allowed access to various restricted areas in the hope that they would present the German side in as favorable a light as possible. Nonetheless, foreign journalists were not completely free in their efforts to inform homeland readers, as there was the constant threat of revocation of their visas if they were too critical in their reporting. An early casualty was Beach Conger of the *New York Herald Tribune* who refused to retract a story unfavorable to the Nazi regime. Others returned home on their own accord, victims of the "Berlin Blues," occasioned by overbearing restrictions.

For Kurt and other Americans in Berlin, the German government's desire to maintain friendly relations with the United States made living in war-time Germany more bearable. At least during his first year of study, other than the general necessity of avoiding sensitive areas, Kurt felt few limitations on his movement within Berlin and Germany. He visited Frederick the Great's palace of Sans Souci in nearby Potsdam, and during the Christmas holidays went by train to Hamburg to be with Uncle Carl's family. While there, he took the opportunity to make a one-day trip to the old Hanseatic city of Lübeck. As much as time allowed he partook of the many amenities and pleasures available to all citizens of the German capital who, except for rationing, black-outs, a ban on listening to foreign broadcasts and shortages of certain items, had yet to witness the full fury of war. Those with sufficient incomes could ignore some of the restrictions on food by patronizing the numerous restaurants in the city which often featured game, poultry and fish on their menus. Attempts to draw attention away from the war contributed, like an opiate, to a booming night life in spite of the black-outs. Nationally, cinema attendance doubled between 1939 and 1940. Operas, concerts and drama productions attracted full houses. Kurt especially enjoyed the performance of Puccini's Madame Butterfly at the Berlin Opera house.

Kurt quickly adjusted to German university life, even though it was thoroughly dominated by National Socialist influences. Physical training was compulsory, unless excused by a medical certificate, and *Rassenkunde* (race science), with its concepts of racial superiority, and geopolitics permeated the curriculum and methods of instruction. While the bulk of the teaching faculty did not actively oppose the Weimar Republic, as Germany's governmental system between 1919 and 1933 was called, they were indifferent to its survival, and when the Nazis assumed power, most accepted the new order as a possible regenerative force. Because of their nationalistic leanings, only about ten percent of academic personnel, primarily Jews, Social Democrats and liberals, were dismissed from their jobs. Among those lost, however, were some of Germany's greatest minds, and the integrity of the curriculum was further undermined by the Nazi state's general denigration of intellectualism. Yet, academic life remained somewhat freer than other areas, and as many as 41 of 337 articles which appeared in the *Historische Zeitschrift* between 1933 and 1943 had a distinct anti-Nazi flavor.

Berlin was the largest university in the Reich in 1939 with 12,000 students and 895 professors and lecturers. It had long been popular with American students, but their ranks had been rapidly thinned, first by the anti-Semitic policies of the National Socialist regime, which cut Jewish-American attendance. Then, adverse American public opinion, currency revaluation, the threat of war, and, now, the war itself, caused American students to select other places for their foreign study. Traditionally,

Americans had been the largest foreign student group in Germany, but their numbers dropped from 800 in 1932 to only 166 by the summer of 1939 to fall behind ten other national groupings. Large numbers of *Volksdeutsche* (ethnic Germans) from eastern European states and students from southeastern Europe and Turkey, where Germany hoped to expand its influence, were also attracted to the German universities. Of all possible study locations in the Reich, Berlin was the most sought after.

Kurt developed a small circle of friends from among those students especially attracted to him because of his being American. His fluency in German concealed his nationality from most students, but his professors seemed to be aware of it. He learned quickly to employ the Nazi salute, which sheltered him from otherwise "unproductive" explanations, but ultimately joined in the general laxity in its use. Berliners, in particular, held to their traditional "*Guten Tag*" in greeting one another.

No one influence seems to have drawn Kurt to the German cause. Even before coming to Berlin he was in general sympathy with Germany's efforts to alter the boundaries imposed on her in 1919 and to regain her position as a world power. He, therefore, found few occasions to raise embarrassing questions about the conduct of German foreign policy or its history, and thereby bring attention to himself. When he did hold contrary views, he was careful in the manner in which he expressed them; he felt some apprehension that if he appeared too critical, he might be expelled from the University or have his visa rescinded and be sent home. But usually his professors were quite open and understanding. As members of the National Socialist Lecturers' Association (*NS Dozentenbund*), they were well-trained to deal with a wide range of sensitive issues, whether posed by a German national, a *Volksdeutsche* or a foreign student such as Kurt.

In the United States Kurt had occasionally read the pro-Nazi newspaper, *Deutscher Beobachter*, which was printed in New York, but he never joined the German-American Bund, nor did he try to procure Nazi propaganda materials from available sources.

Prior to his arrival in Germany, Kurt knew full well that Germany was a dictatorship and that it often used harsh measures against nonconformists and groups the regime didn't take a liking to; however, he had little real understanding of the political and psychological underpinnings of the regime. His early fascination with the German dictator blinded him to the Third Reich's excesses, and he accepted Hitler's actions rather uncritically. Because he wanted so much to believe the best of the Hitler dictatorship, he became highly receptive to National Socialist influences once he was removed from his ties with home.

While the general milieu in which Kurt found himself in the United States was not conducive to identification with the National Socialist movement, in the closed German society of the period there were few countervailing forces to challenge the influences impinging upon his impressionable young mind. There was strict censorship of the media, and Germans heard, read and saw only what the regime considered acceptable. Propaganda techniques had been highly refined by propaganda minister Dr. Paul Josef Goebbels and his staff to inform, educate and deceive, if necessary. While American films were shown and American novels such as *Gone With the Wind* were popular and still available in bookstores, there was a noticeable absence of foreign newspapers and news magazines offering alternative points of view.

About the only American magazines being sold on the newsstands carried detective and romance stories, hardly a threat to the Nazi state. The few American newspapers that got through the mails were usually several months old and of little current value.

Kurt, unlike other Berliners, had the opportunity to obtain information from the American Embassy; however, because he was disregarding the August directive to leave Germany, he was reluctant to make use of this resource. He also observed the ban on listening to foreign radio broadcasts. Long prison sentences were being given to those defying the ban. Moreover, the few souls who dared to question state policy, such as the worker who, according to German police sources, tried in October, 1939 to induce several German workers to lay down their tools in an armament factory to protest the war, were promptly executed. Reports of the harsh punishments of those who strayed from complete obedience were usually enough to gain conformity from the broad population, Kurt included.

Kurt was also denied the open exchange of views which characterized American campuses and political life. There were no Communist, Social Democrat or Center Party student organizations at the University, only Nazi-dominated ones. "Open" discussions on questions of current interest to foreign students, such as "Germany's Peace Aims" or "The Foreign Anti-German Propaganda Campaign," were organized by the Humboldt Haus. However, they were usually presided over and dominated by distinctly pro-Nazi individuals who used the occasion to propagate the views of the regime. Students and German citizens with whom Kurt had contact, with few exceptions, were hesitant to discuss internal politics or to wander far from the accepted party line, for fear of being overheard. An atmosphere of mutual suspicion seemed to control every conversation. Even Uncle Carl, who had earlier indicated concern that Adolf Hitler's policies might lead to war, now resigned himself to the fact of war and refrained from voicing any opinion which suggested non-support. He couched his true feelings about the war in the expressed hope that an end to hostilities could be found. He had little doubt that if the war did not end soon, it would erupt into something quite different from the four years of trench warfare that he personally experienced on the Western Front a generation earlier. The possibilities of aerial and mechanized warfare had already been demonstrated in Spain and in Poland. In contrast to the 1914-18 war, which witnessed no fighting on German soil, German cities, he felt, would not be spared this time if the *Sitzkrieg* heated up. Neither he nor anyone else at the time could contemplate the destructive power of a fire storm initiated by aerial bombardment.

While Uncle Carl had serious doubts about the direction Hitler took in September, 1939, he felt helpless to do anything about it. After all, what could any individual, acting alone, do against an all-powerful state? He was well aware of what might happen to him if he took a stand against the regime or even came under suspicion. Only the army or a group of high ranking party members could possibly alter the course of events, he felt. He was not unlike thousands of other Germans who reconciled themselves to their fate, hoping for a reprieve, or at least a quick victory which would end hostilities at minimal cost to themselves and their country.

Other than noting that Hitler had brought order and a degree of prosperity to Germany, Uncle Carl contributed little to the transformation which was gradually taking place in Kurt's mind. But neither did Uncle Carl's demeanor inhibit the change. He had never voted for the National Socialist Party and only after Hitler had gained total power did he resign himself to the regime. He avoided all active involvement in party activities. On the other hand, he never publicly did or said anything which could possibly arouse suspicion.

Unable themselves to convince Kurt to return home, Mom and Dad sought the help of their Hamburg relatives through a series of letters. During the Christmas holidays (1939) Uncle Carl, partially from his own gut fears about the situation and partially from his brother's request, suggested to Kurt that he return home as other Americans had done just to "play it safe." In February, when shortages of coal and extremely cold weather were causing great discomfort throughout the country, raising fears that Hitler might strike out to distract the population with a rash of swift victories, Uncle Carl made a final appeal to his nephew to return home, feeling that he would eventually be drawn into the conflict if he stayed. When this failed, Uncle Carl resigned himself to accepting Kurt's decision to stick it out, and after that did his best to be a "father-away-from-home" for his nephew.

———————————

The most important personal influences on Kurt seem to have been the Schulzes, with whom he boarded, several students with whom he consorted at the University and, indirectly, the person of Adolf Hitler. While Kurt usually prepared his own breakfast and had his midday meal at the University, he almost always had supper with the Schulzes. It was during these evening meals that Kurt had his most intimate contacts with the Schulz family. Herr Schulz, a man in his early 50s with a receding hairline and prominent midriff, had been a soldier in the Great War on the Eastern Front. He had served under General (later Field Marshal) August von Mackensen during the early years of the war and eventually participated in the capture of Kovno and Grodno before being taken prisoner near Riga in 1916. He remained a prisoner-of-war until after the Russian surrender. The experience greatly clouded his opinion of the Soviet Union, and he detested not only their new governmental system, but also the Russian people, whom he considered uncultured and backward. The accord with the Stalin regime did not alter his feelings, and the stiff Finnish resistance against Red Army forces following the November, 1939 invasion gave him great satisfaction.

Herr Schulz was strongly anti-Communist, not only because of his Russian experience, but because of several Communist-led uprisings which had occurred in Berlin. He had personally witnessed the riots, strikes and demonstrations that wracked Berlin in the years immediately following the Great War (including the so-called Spartacist revolt of January, 1919) and the general disorder preceding Hitler's assumption to power. The high incidence of unemployment in the city, which reached 636,000 souls in December, 1932, contributed to the turbulence, and after 1930 there was hardly a day in Berlin not marked by some bloodshed. (However, in spite of the unemployment, Hitler never captured the hearts of Berlin workers, and the city delivered a strong anti-Nazi vote to the last.)

Herr Schulz had personally lost the equivalent of $5,000 (a large sum of money at the time) as a result of the inflation following the French seizure of the Ruhr in 1923, and he constantly stressed the instability of the Weimar years and the failure of the new democracy to provide security and status for those serving it. He had been a minor official in the German civil service and, along with other civil servants, felt his position threatened by the lack of governmental stability during the Weimar period and by attempts of then Chancellor Brüning to reduce salaries and pensions to balance the budget.

He had long been a Nationalist, but in the March 1932 presidential election, fearful of the chaos which he foresaw the country falling into and a possible Communist takeover, he cast his vote for Adolf Hitler for the first time. While he was apprehensive over Hitler's coming to power the next year, he was relieved by the order that was ultimately brought to the country by the new regime. In the tradition of the German bureaucracy, with its reputation for neutral competence, he began to serve the Hitler government much as he had served the Kaiser (before having been drawn into the *Landwehr* in 1914) and the Weimar Republic. He had been trained in accounting and had received two promotions under the new administration.

While the Schulzes had no automobile, they had a comfortable apartment and were proud of the new refrigerator purchased in early 1939. Few were fortunate enough to afford a refrigerator at the time. They were also able to take at least one vacation trip each year.

Unlike Uncle Carl, Herr Schulz was far from neutral about Adolf Hitler. Within days after Hitler's assumption of power, Herr Schulz joined the S.A. *(Sturmabteilung)* and took an active part in Nazi Party activities, though never a leading role. He was too old to get wrapped up in the movement emotionally as did many young people, but he did participate in two of the party rallies at Nuremberg. He became a strong personal admirer of the Nazi dictator, feeling that the German leader had developed in the German people a new pride and greater respect for Germany's place in the world of nations. He continuously denounced the *Diktat* (dictate) of Versailles, which, he felt, had brought such humiliation to his country because of its harsh terms.

"How could anyone believe that Germany had complete responsibility for the Great War?" he would ask. "The French, with their policy of revenge, the Russians, with their desire to control the Balkans, and the British, worried about the rise of Germany as a competitor in world markets and a threat to their dominance of the sea, were the real guilty parties! Imperial Germany was drawn into a war it didn't want. The theft of Germany's colonies and territorial revisions in Europe, including the spiteful Polish Corridor, were bad enough, but on top of that, Versailles (Article 231) required Germany to accept full responsibility for all the loss and damage to which the Allied and Associated governments and nationals had been subjected as a consequence of the war. It was their war, but they just had the misfortune of having had the entire war fought on their soil rather than on German soil. Even had some reparations been justified, the demands were excessive and far beyond Germany's ability to pay."

With that, Herr Schulz felt that Hitler had a perfectly legitimate right to condemn the Versailles *Diktat* and to remove its shackles as soon as possible. As a treaty reached under duress, it could hold up only as long as Germany was weak.

"Germany," Schulz noted, "had no alternative but to remilitarize. She would have been constantly open to reoccupation, as in 1923, had she not rearmed. Do you think the French would have hesitated to move against Germany in 1936 when German forces entered the Rhineland had they not been fearful of Germany's ability to fight back?" he asked. "Germany's eastern policy was based on a legitimate claim to territory formerly or currently occupied by Germans, and Britain and France had no reason to declare war. They were in no way being threatened. Are they willing to sacrifice millions of men over just a possible loss of prestige in not honoring a stupid pledge to the Poles?" Herr Schulz was strongly supportive of the move against the Poles who, he felt, showed such little concern for Germany's legitimate territorial claims.

"There would have been no invasion had they been willing to accept the return of Danzig, which is 95 percent German, to the Reich and to negotiate a settlement which guaranteed German rights in the Corridor. We did not start this war," he would say; "Britain and France did, by backing up Poland. If we had really wanted war with them, do you think we would have held our armies back along the Rhine and refrained from bombing their cities? We want peace and are giving the two powers time to come to their senses. But if they wait too long, who knows what might happen?"

Kurt was greatly impressed by Herr Schulz's self-assuredness, even though his host had little say in the German government. Herr Schulz found a ready listener in Kurt, because many of the things he had to say coincided with what Kurt wanted to believe.

Herr Schulz's almost frantic fear of Bolshevism and its threat to property and western civilization was gradually transferred to Kurt, even though Germany and the Soviet Union were supposedly allies at the time. Schulz's antipathy towards France also gave added support to Kurt's own feelings of hostility towards the French. While Herr Schulz did not want to see a "real" war with France, he wondered how there could ever be cordial relations between the two countries, given the treatment of Germany by the French after 1918. On the other hand, he had great respect for Great Britain and admired Neville Chamberlain, who, he felt, at least until England's misguided pledge to Poland in 1939, had demonstrated a keen understanding of the German position and had attempted, up to that time, to be accommodating in righting some of the wrongs of Versailles. Peaceful adjustment, after all, was the alternative to war. The British had not participated in the 1923 occupation of the Ruhr and had often sided with Germany against France's overbearing policy, including support in 1931 for a customs union with Austria which was bitterly opposed by the French out of fear that it might lead to eventual political union.

Herr Schulz was equally enthusiastic about the domestic policies of National Socialism. He noted that the movement had brought new purpose to both young and old who had lost faith in themselves and in the future. "Before 1933," he emphasized, "the Germans were a confused and humiliated people, living for the moment, mindless of a future which held little promise. Many of the excesses of the 20s were expressions of this intellectual chaos. Now, we know who we are and where we are going! We are again proud to be Germans and are willing to fight those attempting to contain our historic destiny!"

Herr Schulz seemed not to be disturbed by the outbreak of war, as he foresaw an eventual agreement recognizing Germany's occupation of Poland without the present situation escalating into an all-out conflict. Even if it came to total war, he was convinced that, with Russia neutralized, Germany could easily defeat France and Britain. He seemed to have given no thought to an eventual American involvement in the conflict.

Kurt had little need to be convinced by Herr Schulz, since the accountant's comments only reinforced many of the feelings he already held. But this reinforcement was extremely important in opening Kurt up to broader influences. Herr Schulz developed a strong liking for the young American student who listened to him so intently, and he introduced him to other minor government officials and invited him to attend various party meetings.

Being American opened Kurt to numerous conversations, since Germans wanted to know what he thought about the war. More importantly, they were eager to convince the outsider of the justice of Germany's cause. Time after time in those early months of the war Kurt heard the comment that Germany had no quarrel with England, and, although no love was lost over the French, Germany had no territorial ambitions in the West now that the Saarland had been returned to the Reich. In spite of the non-aggression pact concluded with the Soviet Union in August, 1939, the German acquaintances privately gave the impression that the Soviets were the real enemy of the Reich, and that Britain and France, rather than fighting Germany, should make peace and join her in containing the Communist menace from the East. A war which weakened either or both sides could only benefit Soviet Russia. Kurt was reminded of the article in the *Atlantic Monthly* by Charles Lindbergh (given wide coverage in the German press) which expressed a similar concern.

The University environment was also an important influence on Kurt's transformation. Many German students were the children of members of the various professions or of middle grade civil servants who had suffered loss of status during the Weimar years and had various reasons for supporting the National Socialist government. Partially because of this, students as a group provided the Nazi regime with one of its most reliable sources of support. Expanding in numbers from 69,000 in 1914 to 120,000 in 1932, university students became especially susceptible to Nazi appeals when the Depression greatly curtailed the ability of the German state to utilize their talents upon graduation. As early as 1931, nearly three-fifths of all undergraduates gave their support to the National Socialist Students' Association. Upon coming to power, the Nazis quickly halved the university population by instituting a *numerus clausus* and restricting the number of female admissions.

Virtually all students had been members of the Hitler Youth (*Hitler Jugend*) or League of German Girls (*Bund der Deutschen Mädchen*) and had been thoroughly indoctrinated by the regime before they entered the University. Members of the two movements were involved in a multitude of activities which included summer work camps, rallies, parades, sports, and study sessions. These left little room for boredom and gave youth the impression that they were part of a great invincible enterprise to which they were obligated to give their utmost effort and devotion. Group activity and teamwork were promoted and self-sacrifice was encouraged. Young people were told that the strength of the German nation lay in working together for a common goal, for one another rather than against each other as in the pre-1933 period. *Gemeinnutz geht vor Eigennutz* (the common good comes before one's own good) and *Du bist nichts; dein*

*Volk ist alles* (you as an individual are nothing; your country is everything) were popular slogans of the Hitler regime.

Youth was led to believe that in unity nothing was impossible (giving hope for a better future) and that they were unique and superior to other groups. The rallies they attended were like huge religious revival meetings in which the speeches and ceremonies were organized to mesmerize the audiences and elicit strong emotional feelings. The largest of these events, attracting over 200,000 followers, was the annual party rally which took place in September of each year in Nuremberg. It combined stirring speeches by the Nazi leaders, including Adolf Hitler, demonstrations by drum and bugle corps, massed bands, marching units, and *Sprech-Chor* (speech choirs), torchlight parades, banner displays and other rituals designed to evoke enthusiastic response.

The essence of the Nuremberg spectacles was masterfully captured by Leni Riefenstahl in her film *Triumph des Willens* (Triumph of the Will). The rallies have been described as "masterpieces of theatrical art." Those in attendance went through an emotional experience which culminated with the appearance of Adolf Hitler. The massiveness of the display, with its banners, music and torch light parades inspired a sense of unity and irresistible power within participants of all ages.

Much emphasis was placed on physical training, a feature which Kurt found attractive, as he was a fairly good athlete himself, excelling in swimming and track. While at the University he often went swimming, rowing and running with his circle of friends and competed with them against other groups. That he, as an American, sometimes won the 100 meter dash and broad jump was not disturbing to them, for after all, he was a misplaced Aryan, having been born in America only by an accident of history.

Kurt was also drawn by the regime's attitudes toward heavy eating, drinking and smoking. Kurt neither smoked nor drank hard liquor; he occasionally drank beer with his German comrades, but always in moderation.

A close friendship developed between Kurt and Hartmut Hedwig, the son of a lawyer who was also a leading Nazi activist in Berlin. Hartmut had met Hitler personally and through his father had also met many high ranking Nazi officials, including Rudolf Hess. His enthusiasm for the Nazi regime bordered on the exuberant. Kurt was often invited to the Hedwigs' comfortable villa in Dahlem, where the father took great satisfaction in boasting about Germany's latest triumphs in front of the young American. On Kurt's first visit in late October it was about the sinking by a German submarine of the British battleship Royal Oak in Scapa Flow and the collapse of Poland after only three weeks of fighting. On the occasion of Kurt's second visit, shortly before the Christmas holidays, the boast was about the liner Bremen's successful return from Murmansk after having run the British blockade along the Norwegian coast. Because of these successes, Herr Hedwig's confidence in Germany's ability to win the war seemed boundless. But he was a good host and was able to provide the most elaborate table, in spite of rationing, with service from house personnel fit for a king! Hartmut explained that his father hunted several times a year in Bavaria and that the elk brought back were butchered and kept under refrigeration, along with other items, in a unit in the basement. The Hedwigs maintained a groundsman, butler, cook, maid and cleaning lady on the premises to help take care of the thirteen room villa and gardens.

Hartmut had joined the Hitler Youth Movement in 1931 at the age of 14, nearly two years before Hitler came to power. He was influenced by his father, who was an early admirer of Adolf Hitler, attracted by the Bavarian's fiery nationalism and promises of order and dignity for the German people. Herr Hedwig was fearful of losing the family estate he had inherited from his late father, as well as his status, if the Communists came to power or if the country fell into anarchy. He was unwilling merely to sit back to see what would happen, and he became an active participant in the emerging National Socialist Party. It was inevitable that the father's fervor would rub off on his son. Likewise, Hartmut's zealousness influenced Kurt, who was drawn into many of the party activities in which Hartmut participated.

On one occasion Kurt was introduced to Herman Göring who made himself more accessible to the German people than did Hitler. While Kurt found the huge hulk of a man somewhat repugnant, he was, nevertheless, flattered at having been able to meet the Reichsminister. Kurt ultimately found himself attending the scheduled meetings of the National Socialist Students' Association and being accepted as one of them.

———————

But Luther Bachmann, son of a Lutheran pastor, presented a different influence. Afraid to speak openly about politics with other German students, Luther confided to Kurt, for whom he felt a special trust, some of his innermost feelings about the Hitler regime. Luther had been a member of the Hitler Youth and a willing participant in its activities and goals. His father had attended the University of Berlin just prior to the 1914-1918 war, and it was natural that Luther do so also.

His father, whom Kurt met on several occasions, had a pastorate in a small town near the pre-1939 Polish border, having been forced out of his earlier home in Upper Silesia as a result of the 1921 plebiscite which went in favor of Poland. While his father had little liking for the Poles and found theological justification for some forms of armed conflict, he was opposed to the use of military force to change the German-Polish border. He blamed Hitler for being so impatient, because he felt that, given time, Poland, under the burden of mobilization, would have broken down and made major concessions favorable to Germany without war. But he also criticized Britain and France, holding that their guarantees to Poland had indirectly precipitated the war by strengthening Polish resolve to resist making concessions which otherwise would have been forthcoming.

The elder Bachmann supported the idea of a new Poland being resurrected with different boundaries and perhaps an outlet to Gdynia with rights of passage through the existing corridor. As an alternative he saw the drawing of a replacement corridor to the east of Königsberg with an outlet on the Kurisches Haff, completely eliminating the bifurcation of Germany. Participation of the Soviet Union in the partition, he knew, complicated such a reorientation.

Pastor Bachmann was likewise appalled by the atrocities being committed in Poland in the name of order maintenance. Even the German army was upset over these needless killings by the secret police, acting on orders from Himmler. The pastor was a man of God, but he was not free to speak his mind from the pulpit; members of the clergy were not immune to arrest. Yet, he demonstrated considerable courage in a sermon preached the last week of November, 1939 (at which Kurt was present) when he asked his parishioners to remember that the Poles were also children of God, "humans, just as you, and should be treated as such. It was not God's plan to divide human beings into superior and inferior creations. Polish people may appear to be less cultured, less sophisticated, but all of us are equal in the eyes of God and to be recognized as such. There are no favored people." Pastor Bachmann also passed on to his son the love of inquiry and a sense of justice, especially the idea of a *Moral Staat* (moral state) under law.

Kurt found Luther to be exceptionally intelligent and a perceptive, probing individual, quite willing to discuss with him a wide range of issues. Such discussions were not often possible with other University colleagues who had either been thoroughly indoctrinated in the rightness of the Nazi stand on issues or feared being reported to the authorities. Through his father, Luther had access to information that was not available in the closely-controlled media. It was through Luther that Kurt obtained inside information about the newly established concentration camps. Kurt had thought that they were primarily for individuals who were openly opposed to the regime and had to be confined for security reasons. But Luther had evidence to demonstrate that these camps were housing thousands of Germans for reasons unrelated to security, and that large numbers of Jews were already being sent from the Reich to eastern Poland for no reason other than that they happened to be Jewish.

Kurt expressed concern, but could not conceive what these mass deportations might lead to. Although he had read in the New York papers before coming to Germany about the *Kristallnacht* riots against Jews and their property, he had thought that the accounts were exaggerated because of the Hitler regime's general unpopularity in the United States. Because these occurrences affected neither his relatives, his closest circle of friends, nor himself, he, like many Germans, remained insensitive to the problem. Luther, however, could not accept this moral indifference. He asked why a supposedly secure state, supported by the vast majority of the German people, had to resort to group terror. There had been dictatorships in the past, and individuals who appeared to be a threat to the State were often locked up and sometimes killed. But it made no sense, Luther felt, for individuals who posed no threat, who had done nothing illegal, to be rounded up. He was afraid that many of the most important decisions were being made outside of Hitler's purview, and that the Führer was being forced to acquiesce to them after the fact. In particular, Luther had in mind the activities of Gestapo Chief Heinrich Himmler. Already he was wondering what he, as an individual, could do to protest these actions. "Would they stop if the German public were more aware of them?" he would ask. He feared that if not stopped, what now happened to only "some" people might ultimately happen to "any" people. Moreover, Luther was concerned over the impression people outside of the Reich might have of the German people as human beings and as Christians.

Luther was to remain a close friend of Kurt's throughout their student days in Berlin, even though Kurt became more and more drawn into the circles of those supportive of the National Socialist state and its policies.

———————

Kurt never developed a close friendship with Günter Schade. For various reasons this odious, lanky, spectacled individual took a special interest in him and was a continual annoyance during Kurt's stay at the University. Avoidance was difficult since Günter was enrolled in several of Kurt's classes and participated in many of the activities to which Kurt was drawn. What made Günter so obnoxious to Kurt were his constant questioning and sarcastic inferences, almost as if he were a Gestapo agent and not a fellow student.

"Why did you come to Germany to study?" "Why did you pick Berlin?" "What do you think of the policies of the New Germany?" "What are your personal opinions of our Führer?" "Is there an ulterior motive for your involvement in so many student activities sponsored by the Party?"

After the fall of France and the enaction by the U.S. Congress of legislation which could be aimed only at Germany, he asked, "What do you think of your President's unfriendly posture towards Germany?" "Why don't you return to America, or are you trying to escape the new draft law?"

Schade's inventory of questions seemed endless, and, even though some were probably quite appropriate, Kurt was irritated by them; he usually gave evasive answers, not wishing to be drawn into an unnecessary argument which the questioner seemed anxious to provoke. On several occasions a physical confrontation was prevented only through the intervention of Hartmut or other of Kurt's German friends who had no great liking for Günter. Luther, after one near confrontation, explained Günter's behavior as reflective of the general suspicion of foreigners and of people who were "different," an attitude which the regime and its policies tended to engender.

Kurt was informed by friends that contrary to his own suspicions, Günter's father was not a member of the secret police, but a rather meek individual, the owner of a small dress shop on the Kant Strasse. It appeared that Günter, troubled by his father's seeming lack of assertiveness, was playing out a role more acceptable to the New Germany. Kurt wondered how many more there were like Günter. Kurt went to great lengths not to create unnecessary suspicions, and, as his sympathies were with the Reich, felt affronted by Günter's challenges. In spite of Kurt's efforts, Günter's demeanor toward Kurt was to continue on to the day Kurt joined the Wehrmacht, and Kurt was not surprised when he learned in a letter from Hartmut in 1942 that Günter had taken a position with the secret police following completion of his studies in Berlin.

---

Kurt selected Berlin for his studies because it was there that the major decisions of the German state were being made. He also hoped to see personally this new leader of the German people, who, in such a short span of time, had transformed the Reich from a weakling into a major power, feared and respected by other countries. He had heard Hitler on the radio and seen him in newsreels and in the film presentation of the 1934 party rally in Nuremberg. Through these sources he was well aware of the dictator's charismatic powers — his ability through highly emotional speeches and hand gestures to work up his supporters into an hysterical frenzy.

Hitler had early sensed the German people's strong desire for order and renewed respect for their nation. He had attacked the Treaty of Versailles and the policies of the victorious Allies when others had feared to do so. He was able to capture the feelings of millions of Germans who were frustrated by the inability of the Weimar Republic to satisfy their desire for political stability and economic security. He employed a strong nationalistic idiom, fostering the spirit of national self-confidence. His boundless energy and strong determination were characteristics which appealed to Kurt.

But there was more than the spoken word to inspire audiences. The distinctive uniforms, the banners, often emblazoned with the swastika, parades and mass meetings created the impression of belonging to a great, dynamic movement destined to push aside everything in its path. The movement fostered loyalty to country and comrades and hatred of enemies, both internal and external. The call to sacrifice one's own self-interest for the greater glory of the Fatherland also proved a powerful attraction. The salute had the culminating effect of placing everyone under the authority of the leader.

The German totalitarian state was a product of technological developments and unique historical forces which facilitated the manipulation of a large portion of the Reich's masses. The advent of radio and talking films provided Nazi leaders with two powerful instruments of mass communication not available to earlier tyrants, enabling them to reach every village and household with a uniform message. The party became the meeting place of those who feared declassment, of those who sought escape from an unwanted self through identification with an exalted cause which promised action and the hope of restoring German dignity. Still others found the freedom of the modern democratic state burdensome and sought escape through submission to an autocratic leader who could make decisions for them.

Advances in air and ground transportation at once increased the mobility of the military and made possible the rapid deployment of internal security forces to any place in the Reich where circumstances warranted. What allegiance could not be solicited through mass activity and messianic appeal could be achieved through fear and terror.

Kurt had planned to attend at least one of the Nuremberg rallies during his stay in Germany, giving him the opportunity to witness Hitler in his finest moment, but the war led to cancellation of the rallies beginning with the September, 1939 event. Had he been in the right place at the right time of day, Kurt could have viewed the Führer riding through the streets of Berlin on his way to address the Reichstag at the Kroll Opera House on September 1, 1939, following the beginning of hostilities against Poland. But the newcomer to Berlin would have found the occasion cold and uninspiring, as most of those who watched the procession of automobiles only stared in bewildered silence. Thereafter, the German leader strictly limited his public appearances; as he became more and more preoccupied with the war, he spent less and less time in Berlin. He even passed up the traditional May Day Celebration (May 1, 1940) for the first time since coming to power in 1933, even though it coincided with the German triumph over the British at Trondheim in Norway.

Victory over France in 1940, however, demanded a celebration such as Berlin had not known since the beginning of the war, and this gave Kurt his first opportunity to see Hitler in person. A public holiday was called, stores and factories were closed and tens of thousands of Berliners turned out to cheer, Kurt included. American correspondent Howard K. Smith, who was assigned to Berlin at the time, called the occasion one of real, uninhibited enthusiasm, with Germans weeping and laughing from pure, spontaneous joy. Large numbers of small swastika flags were distributed to the spectators and larger, swastika-inscribed banners, some 40 feet long, hung from the buildings along the parade route. Columns of marching soldiers and dozens of military bands inspired the crowds. The climax of the observance came with the passing of the Führer, marked by a swelling of cheers, the waving of thousands of flags and a mass of humanity pushing against the police cordon. Kurt was quickly caught up in the sea of emotions which surrounded him, feeling himself as one with the frenzied mass, drawn by a powerful new force which appealed for support to the heart rather than the intellect. The rapturous enthusiasm of the crowd was generated as much by the hope that an end to the war might now be found as by the pride of having avenged the defeat of 1918. A major announcement by the German leader was expected in the next few days, and Berliners prayed that it would lead to the peace that they wanted so much.

---

Hitler presented his long-awaited peace proposal on July 19, 1940, in a speech to the Reichstag. In what appeared to be a sincere gesture, Hitler indicated that he saw little reason for continuing the struggle, and that he felt it his duty to appeal once more to reason and common sense. He was not speaking as the vanquished begging favors, but as the victor speaking in the name of reason. He was grieved to think of the sacrifices which the war would claim and wanted to avert them. American correspondent William Shirer, describing the 1940 event, noted that "the Hitler we saw... was the conqueror, and conscious of it... He offered peace... But, of course, it's peace with Hitler sitting... astride the

Continent as its conqueror." The maneuver, according to Shirer, was calculated to make it look like England's fault should the war go on.

Kurt was excited over the speech, which was broadcast throughout Germany, for the coming of peace would vindicate his decision to remain in Germany against the will of his parents and the end of hostilities would open up the possibility of their being able to make a delayed visit to Hamburg to celebrate the 30th anniversary of their emigration to America. Hamburg had been bombed 21 times since the first air strike on May 18, but damage had not been appreciable, and, with peace, would not interfere with a possible visit.

Hitler's peace proposal occasioned one of Kurt's longest and most optimistic letters to us, although by the time we received it several months later the war had taken a distinct turn for the worse. We were surprised that the letter was able to get through German and British censors, but that might have been due more to timing than to the content of the letter.

In his letter Kurt expressed how relieved he was that an end to hostilities seemed to be at hand. He acknowledged that the prior three months had been very trying for him, especially when it appeared that the collapse of France would bring the United States into the conflict, ending all chances for peace and resulting in his internment. He hoped that the United States would never become involved in a war with Germany for he felt strong attachments to both his native country and to the homeland of his parents. With a peaceful settlement appearing possible, Kurt indicated his determination to remain in Germany as long as possible.

The attack on Belgium, Holland and Luxembourg had shaken Kurt's confidence in Hitler, for, in contrast to the occupation of Denmark and the incursion into Norway on April 9, 1940, which could be interpreted as purely defensive moves, the march into the Low Countries on May 10, 1940, appeared to be a case of outright aggression. Kurt and several of his German acquaintances were astonished, as the three countries were not at war with Germany at the time and, from what they knew, had gone out of their way to demonstrate their neutrality. Belgium had even refused to admit French or British troops on her soil or to cooperate on defense plans. But the Low Countries had no choice other than to accept the new turn of events, however disturbing. Foreign Minister Ribbentrop called the action necessary to prevent an Anglo-French attack on Germany through those countries. The *Sitzkrieg* had come to a disheartening end!

The invasion again triggered a rash of messages from Mom and Dad who pleaded with Kurt to return home immediately by whichever way possible. Since the scare over Poland, Mom and Dad had tried to correspond with Kurt at least once a month, but letters, having passed through Allied and German censors, were often delayed from two to four months. As long as the Phoney War persisted, there was little evidence of the urgency which had marked the letters sent in September and October, although Mom and Dad continued to pressure Kurt to come home just to play it safe. But, with the war in Europe heating up, correspondence reacquired its earlier perturbed character. Although a number of the earlier escape routes were now cut off, it was still possible to get out of Europe by going through Switzerland and across Southern France to Bordeaux to take the S.S. Washington to New York, or to Lisbon, where either a ship or clipper flight was available. The resumption of hostilities had caught many Americans by surprise. They had been hoping that the protracted stalemate would eventually lead to an understanding. Now they were frantically trying to book space on any ship possible to leave Europe.

Because of German dependence on Swedish iron ore, a large part of which was shipped through the Norwegian port of Narvik, Norway's position in the conflict was of great concern to Germany. Quite legitimately, Hitler feared that the British might seize Norway to stop the flow of ore. While seizure was out of the question for Britain, the mining of Norwegian territorial waters beyond the three mile limit to halt the ore shipments was not, and, on April 8, 1940, the Chamberlain government announced the mining operation. Unbeknownst to Kurt and the German public, the double invasion of Denmark and Norway on April 9, 1940, had been planned for several months under the code name "Weser Exercise," and the German invasion force was already being moved into position several days prior to the mine laying. But Hitler seized upon the operation as justification for the incursion, claiming that he had prevented a British takeover of the two countries. The Nazi Party newspaper *Volkische Beobachter* announced the event with the headlines, "Germany Saves Scandinavia."

While Denmark fell virtually without a struggle, the Norwegians, making use of their more defensible terrain, fought back fiercely. A small British expeditionary force was sent to Narvik and points north and south of Trondheim to bolster the Norwegian resistance. The determination of the defenders nearly caused Hitler to abandon the operation. However, in the long run, Britain, concerned with her own defense (especially after the German move in the west), was unwilling to commit the men, aircraft and naval vessels required to repulse the German invaders, and, after eight weeks of hard fighting, pulled her last forces out of Narvik June 9, 1940. That same day King Haakon and his government, faced with a hopeless situation, ordered an end to organized hostilities.

Other than appearing defensive in nature, the struggle over Norway seemed unlikely to invite American intervention. The German invasion of the Low Countries and France, however, was a different matter, and Kurt feared an eventual American involvement if the war began to go badly for France and Britain. In such an event, he would be interned for the remainder of the war. President Roosevelt's call on May 16, 1940 for the building of 50,000 planes a year and the immediate delivery of supplies to the Allies gave credence to speculation during the latter part of May that the United States would enter the conflict, and a break in diplomatic relations seemed imminent. But the rapid advance of the German armies meant that any help would be too late unless the Wehrmacht could be stopped or slowed down.

Utilizing both airborne and motorized forces, the Germans overran Holland in five days. So swift was the deployment, the plans to inundate the land with water, an ancient defense technique of the Dutch, was not carried out. Queen Wilhelmina fled to England to set up a government in exile. The German push on the same day into Luxembourg and Belgium met with similar success. In spite of the hilly and woody terrain, the Germans, with exacting precision, took the great Belgian fortress of Eben Emael at Liege in two days, breached the defense line along the Albert Canal and broke through the Dyle southern defense system. Within eight days Brussels had fallen, in contrast to sixteen days after the 1914 invasion. In spite of French and British reinforcements, the rapidity of the German advance prevented the Allies from consolidating their positions, and Belgium was surrendered by King Leopold on May 28.

Militarily, the drive through the Low Countries enabled the Wehrmacht to skirt the French fortifications along the Franco-German border, more commonly known as the Maginot Line, and to enter France along its more vulnerable northern frontier. Control over the area afforded greater protection for Germany's vital industrial area, the Ruhr, from land or air attack. On the day of the invasion of Belgium and Holland Winston Churchill replaced Neville Chamberlain as British Prime Minister.

Britain, which had troops in France since September 4, 1939, had committed only ten divisions to the Continent, assuming that the much larger French army, behind its massive fortifications, would be able to hold back any invading force until reinforcements could be landed. But no effective line of resistance was maintained. In 1914, the French army, calling on its reserves, had stopped the German forces short of Paris in the First Battle of the Marne. But there was to be no repetition of the futile war of attrition which marked the 1914-18 conflict. In 1940 lack of resolve and treachery on the part of Vice Premier and World War I military hero Henri-Phillipe Petain and others, who distrusted the British and blamed them for drawing France into a war she did not want, undermined the defense effort.

With the capitulation of the Belgian army and the deterioration of the Sedan-Abbeville-Calais front, the British decided to disengage themselves from the Continent to prevent almost certain annihilation.

Between May 28 and June 4, 1940, some 336,000 men were transported from the beaches of Dunkirk to England in hundreds of small craft, saving a large portion of the British Expeditionary Force and a smaller number of Belgian and French troops (but losing most of their equipment and heavy guns) in one of the largest rescue operations of the war. Although a devastating military defeat, the successful evacuation of her forces from the Continent provided the British with a limited moral victory around which the myth of an heroic episode could be developed. Apparently still hoping for an understanding with the new Churchill government, Hitler did not press his advantage, and the German armies turned south to complete the conquest of France. With her forces in disarray, France lost the capacity to defend herself. Paris was declared an open city to spare her from possible destruction and was occupied by German forces on June 14. Italy, with France on her knees, finally entered the war, occasioning the remark by an angered American president that "the hand that held the dagger has struck it into the back of its neighbor." President Roosevelt promised immediate material aid, but was unwilling to go as far as answering French Premier Reynaud's appeal to request a declaration of war on Germany. He knew that, although incensed, American public opinion was still strongly noninterventionist, and that there was little support in Congress for direct United States involvement in the European conflict. Moreover, any move now could have a negative effect on his renomination and reelection bid. Churchill also could offer no help, requiring the remaining RAF squadrons for the defense of the British homeland. Faced with a hopeless situation, Reynaud resigned, and on June 17, 1940, Marshall Petain, convinced of an ultimate German victory over not only France but also over Britain, asked for an armistice. Four days later, France signed the surrender agreement at Compiegne in the same railway car in which the Germans had been forced to agree to armistice terms in 1918.

Kurt greeted the news of the truce with great relief. He felt little compassion for the French who, to him, had treated Germany so unfairly a generation earlier, but welcomed the moderate demands made on France. He was also pleased with the decision of the New French administration to collaborate with the Reich, since it would place added pressure on Britain to seek a settlement while her island and empire were still intact. Neither Kurt nor most Germans desired a prolongation of hostilities, but if Churchill did not sue for peace, they were assured of a quick German victory over Britain through either aerial bombardment, an effective blockade, or, if necessary, an assault across the Channel.

With the end of the war seemingly in sight, Kurt made plans to complete a second year of studies in Berlin. Not only had he saved money by living frugally during his first year, but the funds which had been meant for extensive travel throughout Europe remained unused because of the outbreak of war. Aside from blackouts, air alerts, air raids of limited effectiveness on some cities, rationing of certain items, shortages of textiles and fruits, limitations on travel and insufficient supplies of coal for heating and transportation during the first winter, the war, so far, had extracted few sacrifices from the German people. (Kurt had planned to visit Uncle Carl's family in Hamburg for Easter, March 24, 1940, but he remained in Berlin because of the limited train schedules caused by the coal shortage and pleas by the German government to refrain from unnecessary travel as long as the shortage persisted.) Most industries were working single shifts, vacations were given high priority, there had been no cutbacks in the number of domestics serving affluent German households, and consumer goods were being produced at pre-war levels. Fewer than a half dozen air alarms had interrupted life in the German capital, and up to the end of August not a bomb had fallen in the city proper. There was little real pressure for Kurt to return home.

At the same time, the British were mobilizing every resource at their disposal for the life and death struggle with Hitler's Reich, trying desperately to make up for the deficiencies in their military preparedness which were allowed to develop during the appeasement years.

For nearly a month the world waited in suspense as Hitler calculated his next move. Having outrun his time schedule, he found his armies on the Channel before a definitive invasion plan had been worked out, and he did not, as expected, follow up his victory over France with a quick assault on the English homeland. He also apparently wished to provide time for the British to evaluate their precarious situation in the hope that they could be induced to come to the conference table and make an invasion unnecessary. As captured German documents later revealed, in June and July 1940, not only did Germany lack the necessary craft to undertake a sea-borne operation, but Hitler himself was plagued by indecision. First, he had serious misgivings about amphibious warfare, and the destruction of Britain was not part of his greater design.

Receiving no response from Churchill to peace feelers, Hitler decided after several postponements to make a direct appeal to the British people. He did so on July 19, 1940, in a speech before the Reichstag. While the actions of the British government in the month following the collapse of France seemed to indicate a strong determination to "go on to the end... whatever the cost may be," Hitler, nevertheless, still hoped for a favorable reaction to what was to be his last appeal "to reason and common sense," to spare "an Empire which it was never my (Hitler's) intention to destroy or even harm." When the offer was rejected by the BBC and British press without an official government response, there appeared to be genuine disappointment by Hitler, Ribbentrop and others who had little desire to see the struggle with Britain continue. It was expected that the Churchill government would welcome the opportunity presented by Hitler's initiative, now that Britain stood alone to confront the overwhelming power of the German war machine. The reply seemed incomprehensible in view of Britain's precarious position. Britain's obstinacy caused one German spokesman to remark, "Your Churchill must be mad! The whole world knows we've won the war, but seemingly not Churchill!"

Kurt was especially angered by the rebuff, since it meant a continuation of the war and another delay in the return to normalcy. By dashing the widespread public anticipation of a peaceful settlement, Britain appeared to be the real aggressor. In continuing the war, she would now have to accept full responsibility for the additional carnage which might result. Ironically, the rejection assisted Hitler in keeping the country on a war-time footing, just as expectations of peace were causing the German people to become complaisant and lethargic. Perhaps this was the outcome he sought. In spite of British intransigence, there was widespread feeling that the conflict would yet be over in a matter of weeks. It seemed, at the time, inconceivable that the island nation could, for long, withstand repeated, massive air attacks by the German *Luftwaffe* and the strangulation of her supply lines by submarines and surface raiders such as the pocket battleship Scheer. If this did not bring her to terms, then the threat of invasion or, if need be, an actual sea-borne assault would. During the latter part of the year the German people awaited an invasion of the British Isles and remained confident that the war would end by Christmas.

---

Kurt, in the meantime, was invited to accompany Herr and Frau Schulz on their annual trek to Bad Salzuflen in the Harz mountains, and he left with them on August 15. Bad Salzuflen was a popular retreat for both vacationers and individuals with a variety of ailments. While some, with rheumatism or heart, circulatory and respiratory afflictions sought the curative powers of its warm medicinal spring waters, others, like the Schulzes, came to enjoy the natural beauty of the mountains, streams and forests, to bathe, hike, and experience the charm of the old town with its *Fachwerk* structures. The general calm of the place, the lovely gardens and evening music created a mood of relaxation and relief from the cares of the war. It was here at a dance on August 18, 1940, that Kurt met Erika Schneider, the daughter of a senior naval officer from Kiel. Kurt was quickly captivated by her engaging smile, her striking natural beauty and her self-confidence. Unlike most American girls he had known, she was conversant on almost any subject and demonstrated what he felt to be a genuine interest in him. On her part, other than for Kurt's handsome appearance, she was attracted to him by her interest in America and by the opportunity to speak English with a native. She found in Kurt both a good conversationalist and a good listener. She was quite surprised to meet an American in Germany at the time, as most, except for some students, reporters and diplomatic and consular personnel, had left the Continent.

Erika had just completed her high school studies in Kiel, and planned to go to Berlin in the fall to attend the *Fremdsprachenschule* (School of Foreign Languages) to perfect her knowledge of English and French. Kurt was elated at the chance of being able to see her again and gave her both a University and home (in care of the Schulzes) address. She, in turn, gave him her address in Kiel. Before leaving Bad Salzuflen, Kurt promised to meet her train when she arrived in Berlin if she would write to him indicating the arrival time.

Erika's father and mother also attended the dance, enabling Kurt to be introduced to them. Both were in their early 50s, but Captain Schneider, with his stout build and graying hair, looked ten years older. Rather than remaining indifferent to the young American, Erika's father demonstrated considerable interest in learning more about Kurt's impressions of President Roosevelt's commitment of military assistance to Britain.

"Don't you think your President has gone too far, considering that your country is not at war with Germany? I personally regard it an unfriendly act with possible far-reaching consequences," asserted Captain Schneider. He was obviously annoyed at what appeared to be a growing friendship between the leaders of Britain and the United States, for he reasoned that the war was being unnecessarily prolonged by sustaining the hope of an eventual direct American involvement in the conflict on the side of the English. Captain Schneider could not believe that the Churchill government would have rejected the Führer's July peace proposal were it not for promises of American support.

"The renomination of your President for an unprecedented third term is regrettable. I feel that this war-monger Churchill would do anything in his power to bring the United States into the war, even to the extent of creating an incident, such as sinking an American merchant ship and then blaming it on the Germans, to do so. Didn't the British sink the Athenia at the beginning of the war to evoke hatred of Germany? Roosevelt would fall for this trick; another American President might not. Perhaps the American people will see through his manipulative methods and elect Willkie in November. We have no quarrel with the United States; none with Britain, for that matter! But if Britain wants to continue the war, Germany will ultimately crush her, and, if it can be done quickly enough, all this talk about American intervention will become meaningless," he asserted.

Kurt was disturbed by his President's seemingly unneutral posture, but could not conceive of the British sinking an American vessel as a means of bringing the United States into the conflict. Listening to the Captain, one could easily be convinced that the United States was following an improper and dangerous course of action. But Kurt knew that the specter of the European Continent's being dominated by a single power, and the threat posed by the possibility of a combined British, French and German navy in the Atlantic under Hitler's control, if Britain were to fall, could not help but cause alarm in Washington. He felt, however, that Hitler had no designs on the United States, any more than he had on England, and that he would take no action against America as long as it allowed him a free hand in Europe. Kurt still believed that Hitler's major aspirations were in the East, that he would grant favorable terms to Britain, whether her withdrawal from the conflict came about willingly or through force, and that war with the United States could be avoided. A resolution of differences with Britain, he felt, would automatically end the danger of American involvement. That was why peace with Britain was so important.

Kurt returned to Berlin with the Schulzes in the late afternoon of August 25, 1940. That night, shortly after midnight, nearly a year after the outbreak of war, the center of Berlin was bombed for the first time, ostensibly in retaliation for bombs dropped in the heart of London the evening before. (Several British aircraft had dropped bombs on the Berlin suburb of Babelsberg on the night of June 22, 1940, but the August 25/26 raid was the first instance of bombs falling on the heart of Berlin.) Although little damage was inflicted and no deaths were reported (only 29 of the 81 aircraft dispatched had reached their target), Berliners, who until then had been almost entirely insulated from the war, were noticeably shook up and angered, and the attack became the dominant topic of conversation the next morning. A raid on Berlin necessitated a round trip flight of over 1,100 miles, a large portion of it over German air space, and penetration of two rings of anti-aircraft batteries around the city. But Air Marshal Göring earlier had boasted quite confidently to Berliners that the air defense system would prevent any such intrusion, or his name was Meyer. (Thereafter, the air raid sirens which preceded the bomber attacks became known as "Meyer's Buglehorn.") From the intensity of the anti-aircaft fire, Berlin seemed well-defended indeed, but the barrage was not enough to ward off all aircraft. Kurt and Herr and Frau Schulz, upon hearing the air raid alarm and first roar of cannon fire a little after midnight, rushed for shelter in the basement of their apartment building and remained there until the all-clear signal about three hours later. They got little sleep the rest of the night, uncertain whether the British would return, but in the morning they found no signs of bomb-damage in their immediate neighborhood. What would have been a headline event in an American newspaper was played down in the German press, with only a few lines devoted to the raid.

A second mission was flown against Berlin the night of 28/29 August; ten people were killed. The first deaths from aerial bombardment in the German capital brought charges that the British were directing their strikes against defenseless women and children, while the *Luftwaffe* attacked only military objectives. Propaganda Minister Goebbels called it a "cowardly attack."

There followed nine more strikes against Berlin over the next two weeks, all of light intensity, but upsetting, causing sufficient disruption in the daily lives of most Berliners to finally bring home to them the fact that they were at war. The raids caused Hitler to return to Berlin from his Obersalzburg retreat, and, in a blistering speech in the Sportpalast, to threaten heavy retaliation against English cities for the impertinence of the British "air pirates." Although the Blitz over Britain had begun in earnest on August 13, it was now intensified, with London as the prime target. Through strict control of the media, the German public was kept uninformed of the earlier *Luftwaffe* missions against London and other targets. But, with the first bombings of Berlin, the news blackout was lifted and the raids on the British capital were announced as reprisal attacks.

Göring thought that the air strikes alone would force Britain out of the war and that a seaborne invasion would be unnecessary. In any case, control of the air was an essential prerequisite to a cross-Channel assault. Air fields, aircraft factories, supply depots and the harbors and cities of England were hit time and time again. Although terrible damage was inflicted and over 30,000 civilians were killed by the end of the year, the *Luftwaffe* failed to secure control of English air space or to break the spirit of the British people. Using its limited number of more maneuverable and better armed fighter planes to maximum advantage, the Royal Air Force (RAF) caused the German air arm to pay a frightful price in both aircraft and air crews. The heroic effort of the British fighter pilots provoked Churchill to remark that "never in the field of human conflict was so much owed by so many to so few." Hitler contributed to the British victory in the air unintentionally by concentrating on London instead of on the air bases, enabling the RAF to recover from an almost complete exhaustion of its fighter aircraft inventory.

Failing to gain air supremacy, but still hoping that the continued pounding from the air and threat of invasion would wear down the British and finally force them to come to terms, Hitler first postponed, and then, on September 17, 1940, indefinitely deferred the invasion plan for which he had harbored little enthusiasm from the very beginning. Ostensible preparations for a cross-Channel assault, known under the code-name "Operation Sea-Lion," continued, however, as did the air war over England. This was not only to maintain political and military pressure on the British, but also to prevent the German people from falling prey to smugness and apathy which might threaten the even greater venture Hitler was now contemplating, an assault on the Soviet Union. Once Hitler turned his attention to the East, he was no longer willing to involve himself in the risky gamble of an invasion of the British Isles.

The German masses were not informed of the effective cancellation of Operation Sea-Lion and were led to believe that bad weather had caused the assault to be postponed to the fall or early spring, but that it would be launched eventually if Britain did not remove herself from the war beforehand.

The outfitting of the liners Bremen and Europa went on, invasion craft continued to be assembled on the coast of the mainland, and the bombing of English cities was stepped up, buttressing expectations of an eventual invasion. Britain was perceived as the only barrier standing in the way of peace, and an early victory was hoped for, not because Germans wanted to see Britain conquered, but because conquest now seemed to be the only course to bring about peace.

The embattled island, supposedly on the brink of collapse, continued to strike back. However, the RAF was at the time incapable of launching the massive attacks characteristic of the latter part of the war, using only from 20 to 30 aircraft on most missions. In contrast, the *Luftwaffe* was capable of amassing up to 500 bombers for a single air strike. (The raid which partially obliterated Coventry the night of November 15, 1940, had involved 449 German planes.) While the *Luftwaffe* could utilize closeby air fields in France and the Low Countries to reach its targets, the RAF often had to fly long distances, placing severe limitations on bombloads. Distance was a limiting factor in strikes against Berlin. In general, the attacks on the German capital in 1940 proved to be more of an annoyance than a real threat by forcing Berliners to spend long periods of time in their cellars or in designated public shelters. The bombings were considered a temporary discomfort until Britain could be eliminated from the war.

Although he was strongly devoted to his native America, Kurt found himself during his year of study in Berlin becoming increasingly attached to Germany and its people. . Their hopes and fears were his hopes and fears. The air strikes against Berlin embittered him every bit as much as they did native dwellers in the German capital. He shared their desire for peace and blamed Britain for prolonging the war. He hoped and prayed that an end to the conflict would come soon, for he feared that the longer hostilities continued the greater the risk of American intervention and the need to make a choice between two loyalties. His growing affection for a German girl was now to strengthen his bonds to the Reich and create an additional dilemma as America moved closer to war.

# CHAPTER IV

# The Decision

Erika's arrival in Berlin shortly after the initial air strikes on the German capital made her more apprehensive than would otherwise have been the case had the city continued to be off-limits to RAF bombers. She therefore preferred to reside in Zehlendorf, where she felt safer, rather than in the core where Kurt lived. The additional commuting time was to her a small trade-off for a feeling of greater security.

Kurt met her train, as promised, and, upon again seeing the attractive young German girl, who had so fascinated him at Bad Salzuflen, his immediate inclination was to greet her with a hug and a kiss. But, not wishing to create an issue and possibly destroy a friendship, which he wanted to cultivate, he opted for a more formal greeting. After all, he had known her for only a few short weeks, and he wished to be as proper as possible. He helped her with her luggage, which was checked at the station storage counter, and then invited her to join him for coffee and cake at the Tiergarten. Several bombs had fallen in the Tiergarten during air raids earlier in September and portions of the park were still roped off. So far the British had flown their missions at night, coming usually around midnight, creating a feeling of safety at least during daylight hours and in the early evening. The opera and theaters adjusted their curtain times to enable Berliners to return home by 11:00 p.m., prior to any possible attack.

Erika used this first meeting in a month to indicate to Kurt her desire to practice American-English with him. Her teacher in Kiel had been trained in England and spoke with a pronounced English accent. She preferred the more open American pronunciation, but had had few contacts with Americans since the war broke out. Kurt was more than willing to help her.

Erika had been to Berlin once as a child and could still remember many of the stately buildings of the city, including the Reichstag before the 1933 fire. When she and Kurt finished eating, they took a long walk through the Tiergarten and past the Brandenburg Gate to Unter den Linden, Berlin's most celebrated thoroughfare. Its physical appearance had been altered noticeably by the absence of the magnificent 250 year old linden trees which had lined the central parkway on her first visit and which had been removed during the construction of a new subway line beneath the parkway. Silver limes had been planted in their place, but they were as dwarfs in comparison. The two continued along the wide boulevard, past the many public structures, monuments, hotels and embassy buildings, including those closed by the war, to the University which Kurt was so eager to show his young female companion. He introduced her to several friends who happened to be in the library.

That evening, following a meal at the University, Kurt accompanied Erika to Zehlendorf, where a room had been arranged for her through friends of the Schneiders. Kurt invited Erika to see a film with him on September 25th. They planned to meet at 5:00 p.m. in front of the Zoo station. That night, September 22/23, 1940, the British bombed Berlin for the first time in over a week. This was followed the next night by another raid which damaged the rail line in the northern part of the city. Kurt, in addition to watching after himself, now began to concern himself with Erika's safety.

Although disturbed by the bombings, Erika quickly recognized that a relatively normal lifestyle could be maintained during daylight and early evening hours, however uncertain the hours after midnight might be. Kurt met her coming out of the subway exit and escorted her to the Kurfürsten Damm where they ate at one of the many outdoor cafes which populated the avenue. Because of the limitations imposed by rationing, it was sometimes necessary to get out to have a half-decent meal, however costly. Following supper, the two watched a film at the nearby Capitol Theater. The program concluded early enough for them to stop for refreshments before catching a subway train back to Zehlendorf. The evening had been so pleasant for the young couple that they had nearly forgotten that a war was on. But as they went to catch a train, the *Flieger Alarm* (air raid alarm) began to wail. Kurt and Erika, along with thousands of other Berliners who were caught by surprise by the earlier than usual arrival of the bombers that evening, ran for the nearest shelter. The attack, which elicited a strong response from the anti-aircraft batteries, kept Kurt, Erika and numerous other Berliners underground for nearly five hours before the all-clear siren sounded. All trains were halted for the duration of the raid, so one could only sit and wait.

Although the strike that night was of light intensity, there was always the knowledge that a direct hit could still end one's life, even in sheltered circumstances. But fear of the unknown was partially overcome by the fact that the two young people were together. Shortly after midnight, a jolt, probably from a bomb which had landed nearby, thrust Erika into Kurt's arms, and he held her and kissed her for the first time. Kurt apologized for taking advantage of the situation, only to receive a kiss on the cheek in reply.

There were several hundred people in the shelter with them, but Kurt and Erika related to each other, almost oblivious to the other people's existence. The long wait enabled the two to talk at length about the war and their individual situations in it. Erika noted that she would have gone to England this year to perfect her English had the war not intervened. She would have preferred America, but that would have been too costly, and she might not have obtained permission anyway.

"Then," reacted Kurt, "we might never have met! It's terrible to think that it had to take a war to bring us together. Let us hope that the war doesn't separate us."

"I hope not!" replied Erika. "Father thinks that the war will be over in the spring, but who knows what might happen before then? We could be killed anytime, even tonight, by a well-placed bomb, long before the end of hostilities. What would you do if the United States were to enter the war against Germany?"

The question hit Kurt like a bombshell. It was not that he hadn't thought about the possibility of an American involvement against Germany, but no one had asked the question so pointedly. He had tried to avoid the issue in his mind by convincing himself that it wouldn't happen. He didn't want to think about it, because it would force him to take sides. It was easy for an Englishman or a Frenchman to view Germany as an enemy or for a German to see England as an opponent and Russia as a potential foe. But he had no quarrel with either side. On the one hand, he had his parents, a brother, neighbors, and the friends he had gone to school and college with in America, while, on the other, there were his relatives in Hamburg, his many friends in Berlin, and now a girl with whom he was falling in love. Loyalty involves a pledge of faithfulness, of love and devotion to a particular person or country. Need loyalty be indivisible, or was it possible to be loyal to more than one interest? Diverse loyalties, he knew, were a fact of everyday life, but when interests come into conflict, one is ordinarily forced to take sides. It is the conglomeration of emotional ties and a feeling of well-being that produce attachment, just as alienation from people and institutions causes detachment. Kurt was drawn to both the United States and Germany, and as long as the two remained at peace, he could continue to hold diverse loyalties. But, if a state of war were to break out between the two countries, loyalty to one side would be interpreted as disloyalty to the other. How could he overcome this dilemma? He could not think of bearing arms against his friends and relatives in Germany, any more than he could think about bearing arms against his family and friends in America. There is the deliberate traitor, who would betray his country or those who had befriended him for personal gain or for ideological reasons, but Kurt had no desire to betray either friend or country, even though he knew that in the event of hostilities between Germany and the United States, he would be forced to decide for one over the other. Whatever his decision, it would be interpreted as traitorous or a betrayal by the other side. But, at least for now, Germany and America were still at peace, and he was still free to contemplate a variety of scenarios without any of them having an immediate impact on the direction of his allegiance, and he could answer Erika truthfully by saying that he didn't know exactly what he would do. He hoped it wouldn't happen.

It was 4:00 a.m. before it was safe to leave the shelter and Kurt was able to escort Erika to her residence in Zehlendorf. He, himself, did not return home until nearly 6:00 a.m.; at least he didn't have to report to work that morning as did so many Berliners. Because the British had demonstrated their ability to reach Berlin far earlier than anticipated, the theaters announced on September 26th that from then on they would open at 6:00 instead of 7:30 or 8:00 p.m.

In the weeks that followed, Kurt and Erika saw as much of each other as their study schedules would allow. Erika received great pleasure from her growing fluency in English and often astounded Kurt with her knowledge of certain idioms and colloquialisms. They often took long walks together in the numerous parks and forests which dotted Berlin, visited the Zoological gardens and attended many of the cultural events which continued in spite of the war. They also made maximum use of the two borrowed bicycles which had belonged to the Schulzes' daughters.

One weekend the two helped the Schulzes pick apples from the three apple trees at their *Schrebergarten* (garden plot) on the edge of Berlin near the Havel River. Apples were about the only fruit to survive the severe winter. The last carrots and rutabagas were also dug out of the ground and wrapped in newspaper to help preserve them for later use. The little weekend hut hardly had room for four people, but it did enable the Schulzes and guests to get away from the tumult of the city for short periods of time and to get a feel of nature's good earth. It also provided a welcome supplement to the standard fare of cabbage and potatoes.

As fall turned to winter and the ponds began to freeze over, ice skating became a favorite past time for the two young people. The first snow brought about the possibility of skiing and sledding in the Harz Mountains and areas south of Berlin.

Erika's parents were becoming increasingly concerned over the attention their daughter was showing the young American student, not only because it was limiting her options with German men, but because of the sensitivity of Germany's position regarding the United States. Nevertheless, in November Erika received permission from her parents to invite Kurt to spend the New Year period with her family in Kiel. Kurt had looked forward to such an invitation.

Berlin was bombed infrequently during the remaining months of the year. One air strike occurred while Soviet Foreign Minister Molotov was visiting the capital for talks with German leaders, but up to the Christmas holidays there was little visible evidence of the war in Berlin, and one could walk for miles in the city without seeing any damage. The effects of the raids were primarily psychological, forcing Berliners into shelters or their cellars (which were now becoming more and more uncomfortable with the approach of winter) for extended periods of time. Reporting to work or to the University the morning after such a raid was especially trying.

But there were also some fatalities. On August 29th four men and two women were killed by bombs which had fallen near the Görlitzer railroad station, and on September 5th a policeman was killed by a bomb in the Tiergarten. The most telling casualty of the air strikes, however, in that it involved someone Kurt knew, was the bombing death of the Schulzes' three year-old granddaughter. She had been killed by a bomb which landed in the side garden of her parents' home, but which had not exploded until after the all-clear siren had sounded and she had been put into her bed on the ground floor. Her parents had been in a bedroom on the other side of the house and received only minor injuries from the explosion. Kurt had come to know the little blond-haired girl very well from the many visits she made with her parents to her grandfather and grandmother's apartment. He had even acted as babysitter on several occasions when the Schulzes accompanied their daughter and son-in-law to a play or film and left the child in the apartment. Kurt and Erika attended the funeral. The pastor lamented the growing number of deaths of noncombatants, in this case an innocent little child. Kurt was among those who placed a shovel-full of earth over the young girl's casket. He became especially incensed at the British for thinking that they could win the war by killing helpless women and children after a chance for peace had been given to them.

Meanwhile, several developments, both within and outside of Berlin, were creating complications for Kurt. Although popular sentiment in the United States was still strongly noninterventionist (in spite of its anti-Nazi flavor), the Roosevelt administration was taking certain actions which appeared to be drawing the country slowly into the conflict. In addition to his earlier promise of military aid, President Roosevelt, by executive agreement, announced on September 3, 1940, the transfer to the British of 50 over-age American destroyers in exchange for 99 year leases on naval and air bases in Newfoundland and a number of British islands in the western hemisphere. Two weeks later Roosevelt signed the

Burke-Wadsworth Act, which required all males between the ages of 21 and 35 to register for possible military service, initially set at one year. The destroyer transfer made America a limited participant in the war and would have justified German retaliation, either through breaking of diplomatic relations or a declaration of war, but Hitler had good reason for not wishing to become involved at this time in a war with the United States.

Kurt learned of the provisions of the Selective Service Act first through the German news media and later through a letter from Mom and Dad, who tried to use the legislation, as well as the reported bombings of Berlin, as yet another lever to convince him to return home before all exit routes were closed to him. They felt that with Britain refusing to negotiate a settlement, the United States would eventually become involved.

But it was this very fear of an American entry into the war against Germany that now kept Kurt from returning home. Although already 23 and subject to the Act, he had no intention of committing himself for service against Germany, against relatives and people he considered his friends. He had also become emotionally involved with a German girl and could not think of taking any action which would directly or indirectly harm her or her family, even if it meant violating his obligations as an American citizen. Kurt saw the enactment as being directed solely at Germany, in support of a country (Britain) which had been granted the opportunity to conclude peace under the most favorable terms, but had refused to accept it. While no pacifist, he wanted nothing to do with any action that would cause him to fight Germany, if it came to that.

The signing of the tripartite military alliance between Germany, Italy and Japan (later known as the Axis powers) on September 27, 1940, was yet another source of concern, as it meant that Germany was committed to assist Italy or Japan if either was "attacked by a power at present not involved in the European war or in the Sino-Japanese conflict." This meant to Kurt that an American move to thwart Japanese expansionism in the Pacific could draw Germany into war with the United States. Kurt could not understand why Hitler would want to risk such a possibility. On the other hand, the Pact could be interpreted as a move to keep the United States preoccupied in the Pacific, thereby minimizing her ability to act in the European theater if war were to break out. Or, faced with the combined might of the three Axis powers, the United States might be fearful enough to give Japan a free hand in the Pacific in order to avoid a larger war.

In any case, Kurt did not like the provisions of the Pact, for, if Hitler really expected the war to be over by the end of the year or in the spring, there would have been no need for the alliance. The agreement seemed to recognize that Britain was proving to be a more difficult opponent than anticipated, so that Hitler had decided to weaken her by endangering her far-flung empire. Italy would become a base for operations in the Mediterranean and Japan, a surrogate for actions against Britain's Asian holdings. This meant that not only would the war not be over in the near future, as most Germans were hoping, but that the war might possibly be expanded to other theaters with German forces being sent to locations as distant as Africa and even the Pacific. This was upsetting to Kurt, for the longer the war continued and the more it expanded into other areas, the more likely the possibility that the United States would become involved.

As he walked to the University on the day of the signing, Kurt noticed many German school children carrying small Japanese flags.

Kurt's fear of an irrational move on the part of Mussolini, the Italian dictator, was borne out on October 28, 1940, when, contrary to Hitler's wishes, Italian forces invaded Greece from Albania, a small Balkan country which Italy had seized the previous year. Although he was embarrassed by the action, it was too late for Hitler to do anything about it. The German leader had hoped to neutralize the Balkans without war. Now the Italian incursion invited possible British intervention in the Greek campaign. But the Germans knew that Greece would not be the pushover that Albania was, as a good number of Greek officers had been trained at Potsdam. There was an attempt in the German press to justify the latest Italian move as having been provoked by Greek complicity with the British, but Berliners saw it as an expansion of the war and another obstacle to peace.

Mussolini, apparently wishing to emulate Hitler by building an empire of his own in the Mediterranean, had occupied Albania on April 7, 1939, and in September 1940 invaded Egypt from his Libyan base, assuming that Britain was about to be invaded by Germany and would be unable to reinforce her position there. When the invasion of Britain did not come off, the Duce, as Mussolini was called, seemingly decided to strike out on his own to demonstrate his independence.

It was under the cloud of a possible expansion of the war that Kurt and Erika returned to their respective families for the Christmas holidays. In spite of the air attacks, there were few obstacles to traveling throughout the Reich during this second Christmas of the war. Hamburg and Kiel, however, were much more accessible to the British Bomber

Command than Berlin, because they involved shorter flying distances and their distinctive geography made them much easier to locate. Nevertheless, even with these advantages the British were incapable of launching a significant attack, and on only five occasions did a mission against Hamburg involve more than 30 aircraft. In contrast to Berlin, however, which had witnessed only a dozen or so strikes, Hamburg had been hit 72 times during 1940; the most serious strike occurred on the 15th and 16th of November when 20 people were killed and 1,300 people left homeless. During the year (since the first air strike on May 18, 1940) 125 people had been killed in the bombings. People grew accustomed to the blackouts; they drew curtains and even began to accept the frequent treks to the cellar.

Kurt arrived in Hamburg on December 22. He had not seen Uncle Carl, Aunt Erna and cousin Christina for nearly a year. His planned visit for Easter had been cancelled because of the fuel shortage which restricted rail travel. But what a difference the year had made! Christmas 1939 had been celebrated in the middle of a Phoney War. There had been no bombings of the German cities and consumer goods were still available in such quantities as to make one wonder if there really was a war on. Spirits were high, and food, while not in abundance, was adequate. Kurt had brought along presents he had purchased in the United States for the occasion, including clothing and several items for the kitchen.

This year Kurt had to rely fully on the German market for his gifts. But, as he didn't have to use any of his 150 clothing points for his own needs, having taken a full wardrobe with him from the States, he used them to purchase clothing items for his uncle's family and for Erika. A pair of men's trousers, for example, consumed 20 points, a woman's blouse 15, a woman's skirt 20, and a pullover 25. Even an apron required 12 points. It didn't give Kurt much leeway with two families to please, but the items were very much appreciated by all concerned.

The Schröders attempted as best they could to celebrate their Christmas as they had in the pre-war period with Christmas breads, candies and a candle-lit tree. What Uncle Carl couldn't get on the open-market, he bartered for with exchanges of breads and cakes, and the Christmas eve meal of soup, carp, red cabbage, peas, potatoes and apple cake with whipped cream couldn't have been improved upon even in peace time. The war had prevented Uncle Carl from having his automobile this Christmas, but he realized that it wouldn't have meant much with so little petrol available for private use. The British stayed away during the entire time that Kurt was in Hamburg, adding to the pleasure of the visit.

On December 30, Kurt left for Kiel to spend *Sylvester* (New Year's Eve) with Erika's family. This was Kurt's first visit to the important naval and shipbuilding center which controlled one end of the Kaiser Wilhelm Canal connecting the Baltic with the North Sea. As with other North German ports, Kiel had been bombed on a number of occasions, but none of the raids had been of sufficient magnitude to prove more than a nuisance. Kurt found the city quite beautiful, and much of December 31st was spent seeing the many sights it had to offer, including its lovely fjord. That night the New Year was celebrated with great festivity and confidence. During the year Germany had defeated France, nearly brought Britain to her knees, and was master of Western and most of Central Europe, feats accomplished with a minimum of sacrifice. While there were shortages of textiles, fruit, and some vegetables, the German people still ate well and had sufficient clothing. Their cities were no longer off limits to the RAF bomber groups, but during the year the British took far more from the *Luftwaffe* than they could deliver in return. In spite of the disappointment over the continuation of the war, most Germans expected to witness its conclusion in the New Year, believing that the British could not hold out much longer. Little did they realize what momentous decisions were then being made, decisions which would completely change the complexion of the war in 1941.

In the Schneider's semi-darkened parlor, Kurt sat comfortably in an upholstered mohair club chair next to a long rectangular coffee table which had been set up with a lovely service of Rosenthal china. In the center of the table were several plates full of cakes, cookies, and candies, three bottles each of champagne from France and Mosel wine from Germany. With Kurt, Erika, and Erika's parents were a young naval officer, Lieutenant Kramer, and his wife. Lt. Kramer, who served as Captain Schneider's adjutant, showed considerable interest in the young American, who was about his own age, and expressed astonishment that an American would want to continue to study in Germany when war between America and the Reich was becoming a distinct possibility.

"You surely recognize that the actions of your President may lead to war with Germany? Isn't it rather risky for you to continue to study in Germany under these circumstances?" he asked.

"Don't think I haven't thought long and hard about it," answered Kurt. "I know that the American people don't want to get involved and that Germany has no quarrel with us. If Churchill would only come to his senses and accept a settlement as proposed by the Führer in July, then the war could end very quickly, along with all of this talk about American participation! Hopefully, the war can be brought to an end either through negotiation or by forcing Britain to the bargaining table before the United States becomes even more deeply implicated in what should remain a European matter. I, personally, have a certain reluctance to return, for doing so would subject me to induction and possible service against Germany if my country were to enter the conflict. I just couldn't fight against my relatives and friends," stressed Kurt.

"But that," replied Lt. Kramer, "is one of the facts of life. If you are born an American, you fight whomever the American government tells you to fight against, just as I, as a German, will fight against any country my Führer considers to be an enemy of the Reich. You can't just decide not to fight because you know someone in another country. After all, I spent two months with a family in England during the summer of 1936, and I can only say that they were awfully nice people. But if Churchill sends their two sons against us, then it is my duty to defend the Reich against them. While you are free to do as you please, your argument seems pretty naïve to me. You will ultimately have to make a decision if America continues its unfriendly moves against Germany. Either you will become our enemy or you will have to join us!"

Captain Schneider was quite embarrassed at his adjutant's curt remarks, however much he might have agreed with him, and he tried to turn the conversation to another subject by asking Kurt how his parents felt about his remaining in Germany during these troubled times. "Aren't your parents worried about you? An English bomb is just as likely to fall where you are as on a German."

"Oh, Father," interrupted Erika, "that's not nice to talk to Kurt like that! He's willing to take the risk just as I am and you are. The main thing is that our two countries are not now at war, and we shouldn't talk about what might never happen." The Schneiders knew that their daughter had been seeing Kurt regularly in Berlin, and they wanted to know whether he intended to remain in Germany with the intention of becoming a German citizen, or whether he was contemplating a return to the United States.

"My parents definitely want me to return home," replied Kurt. "Mother has been pleading for me to give up my studies in Berlin ever since last year when Britain and France declared war on Germany. She feels that America will eventually be drawn into the conflict, and that I should leave before all routes of escape are cut off. I guess that, in addition to my unwillingness to be subject to an enactment which would possibly force me to bear arms against Germany, I have had an unconscious desire to demonstrate my independence from my parents. I suppose that I haven't wanted to admit that I have been wrong several times, first in trying to convince myself that there would be no war, and second that peace would come easily."

Erika's parents had mixed emotions over their daughter's interest in the young American student. Not that he was unpleasant, lacked intelligence or appeared to be socially inferior, but that their only child, whom they considered bright and attractive, had given up all interest in two German male acquaintances who could have offered a more permanent relationship. First, the young American could decide to return to the United States any time, leaving their daughter in the lurch. Second, her relationship with him could raise questions of loyalty, particularly if hostilities with the United States were to break out. How could they be certain that he would side with Germany in such a situation? Third, if the relationship were to lead to marriage and the two were to go to the United States just prior to a state of war erupting between the two countries, they might never see their daughter again. They would prefer that the relationship be broken off unless Kurt were to commit himself to the German Fatherland. That would resolve most of their concerns.

The Schneiders had decided to invite Kurt to Kiel over the New Year holidays to get to know him better and to learn more about his intentions. They had tried on several occasions, because of their reservations about the American student, to convince their daughter to break off the relationship. But Erika was unwilling to do so. She considered Kurt to be the first man to give recognition to her own ideas and intelligence and to treat her as an equal. He was kind and considerate and a real gentleman. This was in stark contrast to her two former German boyfriends, whom she considered arrogant, disrespectful and sometimes demeaning. She told her parents that she would be willing to follow Kurt to America if he were to ask her to marry him. The Schneiders, in turn, felt that their failure to recognize their strong-willed daughter's personal wishes, at least to a point, might strengthen her resolve to continue the relationship in order to punish them. So they tried to remain flexible, but were disturbed that Kurt's stay in Germany seemed to be determined as much by his consideration of the anticipated consequences of a return to America as by his interest in the German cause.

At least the short stay enabled them to get to know the young man better. They found him intelligent, polite and understanding of the German cause. He had brought a new sparkle and resourcefulness into their daughter's life. Since going to Berlin her relationship with them had improved, and she seemed suddenly to have grown up. In this sense, the liaison with Kurt, they felt, had been a good influence on their daughter.

---

Unknown to all but a small group of his closest advisors, Hitler, without waiting for the struggle with Britain to be brought to a successful conclusion, began to develop plans for his most ambitious undertaking in fulfillment of a life-long objective, the conquest of the Soviet Union. Documents and personal accounts by people close to him indicate that in this venture Hitler was never troubled by the extreme indecisiveness which characterized his cross-Channel invasion plans. To him coexistence with Britain was considered desirable and achievable, but he was convinced that conflict with the bastion of Bolshevism was inevitable and that a grand crusade to crush her must take place while the Reich was at the height of its power, and before the German people had become complacent and weary of war. He didn't want to risk attack by a more formidable Red Army at some future point in time under less favorable circumstances. Only by Russia's defeat, he felt, could the long-term survival of the German nation be assured.

The relatively effortless victories of 1939 and 1940 had created an illusion of German invincibility. At the same time, German leaders were deceived into believing that the Stalin regime would collapse and the country disintegrate in face of the over-powering might of the Wehrmacht. The ineptness of the Red Army in its David and Goliath dual with Finland, the observed obsolescence of the weaponry displayed at the parade in November 1940 marking the anniversary of the Russian Revolution, and the earlier purges of Russia's military leadership tended to reinforce the perception of the Eurasian giant as a weak and potentially easy victim. Hitler was assured that the operation against the Soviets could be concluded in a matter of months, before the onset of the dreaded Russian winter.

Although Germany and the Soviet Union were parties to a nonagression pact which provided for the settlement of disputes or conflict by friendly exchange of opinion or by arbitration, relations between the two powers, while outwardly cordial, remained strained. Suspicions were early aroused by Soviet designs on the Baltic States which contained large numbers of German nationals. Hitler was especially incensed by the advantage taken by the Soviets in June 1940 when he was preoccupied in France. Without advance notice the Soviets terminated the semi-protectorate status of Estonia, Latvia and Lithuania by outright annexation. This was followed by the Soviet seizure of Bessarabia and Bucovina from Romania, prompting Germany to guarantee Romania's remaining territory in order to ensure access to crucial oil resources. Overlapping interests in Finland, where Germany was strengthening its cultural, economic and military ties, and in the Balkans generated additional mistrust of the Soviet Union. Hitler's tentative considerations of a move to crush Russia seem to have hardened into a definite decision during the November 12-13, 1940 discussions with Vyacheslav Molotov in Berlin, when the Soviet Foreign Minister clarified the extent of Soviet ambitions in the Balkans and the Straits. On December 18, 1940, after four months of preliminary planning, the formal directive for the invasion of Russia, under the code name *Operation Barbarossa* (Operation Red Beard), was issued. The decision to move to the east did not represent an abandonment of the effort to defeat Great Britain; rather, it was viewed as part of a larger strategy to isolate and weaken the island nation's ability to continue the war. Hitler was convinced that British hope of an eventual Soviet attack on Germany was one of the reasons the island nation had refused to accept his several peace offers. Through the elimination of Soviet Russia, the defeat of British forces in North Africa, the pressure exerted on London's lifeline by the war being waged on the high seas against her shipping, and the encouragement given to the Japanese to enter the war against British interests in the Far East, Hitler felt that Britain would be forced "to come to an understanding" before the United States could become a factor in the war.

The German dictator was temporarily diverted from his absorption with Operation Barbarossa by the failure of the Italians in their North African campaign and by unexpected developments in the Balkans. When the British counteroffensive succeeded in driving the Italians out of Egypt and Cyrenica, the German *Afrika Korps* under General Erwin Rommel was sent to Libya to recover the initiative.

Italian units were faring no better in Greece, and by March 1941 they had been pushed back into Albania, where the invasion had been launched the previous October. Germany could no longer remain indifferent to events in the Balkans because of the threat which British air bases in Thrace could pose to Romania and Italy. On March 1, 1941, Bulgaria, Greece's northeastern neighbor, joined the Axis alliance and allowed German troops to enter the country from Romania and to position themselves for a thrust against Greece. Although Russia was informed of the treaty and contemplated troop movements, and was assured that German forces would be withdrawn from Bulgaria as soon as the British had been expelled from Greece, she was disturbed by the fact that Germany had interfered in what she considered to be her sphere in the Balkans.

One aim of Hitler's Balkan policy was to obtain Yugoslavia's compliance without war. This goal appeared to have been achieved by the March 25, 1941 accord which aligned Yugoslavia with the Axis powers. Two days later, however, the Belgrade government was overthrown by a group of officers adverse to the Axis cause; on April 5 they signed a friendship and nonaggression pact with the Soviet Union. So infuriated was Hitler by this turn of events that he was determined, without first resorting to diplomatic measures, to avenge this treachery by crushing the Yugoslav state with "merciless harshness." The invasion was launched at dawn on the sixth of April. To satisfy Hitler's desire for revenge, the Germans systematically bombed the Yugoslav capital city of Belgrade for three days, killing more than 17,000 people. The country was overrun in twelve days and later dismembered.

Simultaneously, German units were sent into Greece, where they faced fierce resistance from Greek troops reinforced by about 45,000 British, Australian and New Zealand soldiers. However, in spite of the tenacious defensive action, Athens fell on April 22nd, and by May 2 all of Greece was in German hands. The island of Crete was taken by German paratroopers during the last eleven days of May. But German losses there were so heavy that Hitler called off the proposed air-borne invasion of Cyprus, and he never again used air-borne forces in a major campaign.

While the conquest of Yugoslavia and Greece enabled Hitler to dominate the Balkans and most of the eastern Mediterranean, it forced him to delay the assault on Russia by a crucial five weeks. Rather than May 15, the invasion was now to take place on June 22, 1941.

Instead of witnessing the long-awaited invasion of England to conclude the war, the spring of 1941 found German forces involved for the first time in operations far away from their homeland and against countries other than England, creating new enemies and new lands to occupy. The expansion of the conflict was unsettling for Kurt and for most Germans, who were becoming increasingly pessimistic over their country's ability to end a war which had begun as a minor encounter in Poland and had now spread to encompass nearly all of Europe.

———————

Kurt felt trapped in the predicament which the rapidly changing international scene was imposing on him. He had woefully misjudged the ultimate consequences of the forces which had been set in motion by the German action against Poland on September 1, 1939, first by refusing to believe that Britain and France would respect their commitment to the Poles, and then by thinking that once war had erupted it could be easily resolved. He had counted on a peaceful settlement, initially after the fall of Poland and then after the fall of France, to enable him to complete his studies and look forward to a normal life, possibly as a teacher of modern history at an American college. But the British were tenaciously refusing to come to terms, forcing Germany to try to undermine her resolve by becoming engaged on a number of distant fronts. Kurt's utmost worry was that the longer the British remained in the war, the greater the possibility of an American involvement.

He was having strong second thoughts about the wisdom of his decision to go ahead with his German study plans at a time when peace in Europe was so uncertain. Perhaps he had been wrong in refusing to return home after the British and French declarations of war, or after the defeat of France at the latest. His failure to perceive what was happening had forced him into this dilemma. Yet he was not sorry for having come to Germany. He had learned a great deal and had made many new friends. His decision had enabled him to meet Erika. Now he could not think of leaving her, and he was certain that her parents would block any attempt she might make to leave the country with him should he decide to depart.

His American passport was scheduled to expire on July 10, 1941, while his student visa was valid only until the end of the summer semester in July, and it could not be renewed. He would have to be out of Germany before the July deadline! But without an exit permit, departure was impossible. The necessity to make a decision about his future was close at hand! Under normal circumstances he would merely have applied for an extension of his passport for an additional two years and tried to obtain a job in Germany. But these were not normal times. Europe was at war, and ordinary Americans were not free to travel in the war zones. His eligibility for American military service, he knew, would be another reason for nonrenewal. Moreover, other Americans were being denied exit permits by the German authorities, and there was no certainty at this time that he would be granted the documents required to leave the country.

In the meantime, the United States was rapidly being drawn into the European conflict. With Britain's financial reserves in America nearly exhausted from arms purchases, Congress, after a bitter debate, passed the Lend-Lease Act in March 1941. The statute gave the President the power to authorize the manufacture and the transfer, sale, exchange or lease of any defense article for any country whose defense he deemed vital to the defense of the United States. Passage of the legislation moved the United States from a friendly neutral to a full-fledged nonbelligerent. At the end of the month, American authorities, on technical grounds, seized 28 Italian and two German ships in American ports. In April, under agreement with the Danish Minister in Washington, authorization was granted to the United States to establish military and naval installations on Greenland to prevent possible German seizure of the island. On May 27, 1941, Roosevelt proclaimed the existence of an "unlimited national emergency," giving him broadened war powers, and in June the German and Italian consulates and information services in the United States were forced to close and their American assets frozen. Like action was taken against American consulates and assets in Germany and Italy.

With America moving closer to war with Germany, Kurt was increasingly concerned with the provisions of the Selective Service Act (1940). He was of conscription age and felt that if he failed to return home within a reasonable period of time, he would be charged with draft evasion. The draft proclamation had stipulated that a person not within the continental United States on October 16, 1940, "shall within five days after his return. . . present himself for and submit to registration." Failure to do so would subject the individual to fine or imprisonment or both. Although no time limit for the return was established, Kurt feared that even if he could now leave Europe, he would have difficulty explaining the long delay and be imprisoned for his inaction.

On the other hand, if he were to return and was inducted without trouble, he would dread the possibility of having to take up arms against Germany at some future date. Not only was there the question of diverse loyalties, but also concern for Erika, her parents, and friends and relatives in Hamburg.

After the July 10th expiration of his passport he would be in Germany illegally, subject to expulsion or detainment. He had to come to a decision. For some time he had thought about the possibility of becoming a German subject. As the son of German-born Protestant parents, he anticipated few problems, even with a regime harboring such extreme racial and religious policies. The possibility had been suggested to him by his student friend, Hartmut Hedwig, whose father had numerous connections in Berlin, and, indirectly, by Erika's father. Under normal conditions the decision would be rather simple. It would be little more than a son returning to his parents' country of origin. It happened all the time. But these were not normal times, and Kurt had to consider the reactions of his parents and brother, as well as of those with whom he had grown up. It was not just a matter of becoming a German, but of becoming a supporter of a system that was widely despised in America. While there were aspects of the Hitler regime which he didn't approve of, he felt strongly that once the war with England was over and the regime felt itself more secure, its more repressive elements would be discarded and it would evolve into a traditional dictatorship without the excesses which currently characterized it.

But considerations of the character of the regime were now being pushed into the background by the rapidly deteriorating relationship between the United States and Germany. As a result, Kurt was hesitant to forsake his native country, in spite of his support for the German cause. In addition to concerns for his parents, he did not want to place himself in a position where he might, by his action, have to fight against the United States. This was as repugnant to him as having to fight against Germany. How he hoped for some spectacular change of events which would bring a quick end to the war! The report of the sensational flight of Rudolf Hess, deputy party leader and second in succession after Göring, seemed to offer a ray of hope. On the night of May 10, 1941 Hess flew to Scotland, where he was arrested and imprisoned by British authorities. But nothing came of the incident, and Hitler, apparently unaware of Hess' mission, disavowed his former devoted follower, concluding that he had become mentally deranged. (Hess, on his own initiative, apparently hoped to conclude peace between Germany and Britain and, through this dramatic coup, regain his former status with Hitler.)

The passage of the Lend-Lease Act and other actions precipitated a hate campaign against the United States, creating new difficulties for Americans still residing in Berlin, particularly those who could speak only English. The earlier friendliness and understanding was now replaced by anger and resentment, and some Americans were forced to vacate their apartments to make room for war workers flocking into Berlin. As the summer semester began, Kurt recognized a distinct coolness and even avoidance on the part of some students ι

counted as good friends. Günter Schade increased his harass

renewed vigor, even spreading rumors that Kurt was a spy. Fo

the Schulzes, Hartmut, Luther, and a few others stood by Kurt, a.

he and three other American students were picked up by the Gest.

questioning, it was through the intervention of Hartmut's father,

called the apprehension a stupid mistake, that Kurt was quickly relea

One of the other students, however, was held in the Alexander P.

prison for two months even though he was never charged with a crim

Although Kurt couldn't be certain, he suspected that Günter Schade hat

somehow precipitated the incident. The American news commentator

Richard C. Hottelet was seized for other reasons and spent several

months in prison before being freed in August 1941. His arrest served

notice to other reporters that they were welcome in Germany only as

long as their stories were acceptable to the Hitler regime.

———————————

Kurt had long considered war with the Soviet Union a distinct

possibility. Despite outward signs of friendly relations between the two

countries since the signing of the nonagression pact in 1939, Kurt was

continually reminded that Germany's real enemy was in the East. The

Soviet attack on Finland and seizure of the Baltic States and portions of

Romania were grim indicators of Soviet Russia's aggressive intentions

and the threat, he felt, she posed to western civilization. Kurt had

developed strong personal feelings against the Soviets, not only because

of the influence of Herr Schulz, Herr Hedwig and others on his thinking,

but from what he considered the geo-political threat to Germany posed

by the menacing giant to the East. While an eventual clash between the wo powers appeared highly likely, Kurt never envisioned himself becoming personally involved in the struggle. It was something he foresaw occurring probably in 1943 or 1944, after Germany had consolidated her position in Western and Eastern Europe and driven Britain out of North Africa, or after an accord had been reached with Britain. He anticipated an ultimate victory against the politically unstable and militarily weak Eurasian giant, but wondered how, over the long run, Germany would be able to hold such a vast expanse of territory, unless it were dismembered into numerous smaller parts.

It was difficult to keep the massive build up of forces on the eastern border areas a complete secret, but an imminent rupture did not seem at hand. The German nation had not been mobilized for war. The Soviets continued to fulfill their economic obligations under various agreements with considerable punctuality, and they were careful to avoid any unnecessary provocation. Germany, in turn, filled orders placed by the Soviets for German goods and maintained deliveries up to the last minute. Yet, there were little signals such as the removal of pro-Soviet books from German bookstores and cancellation of leaves of soldiers stationed in Poland that seemed to indicate that something momentous was at hand.

Germans awoke the morning of the 22nd of June 1941 to learn that their Führer had ordered the Wehrmacht into Russia as a countermeasure against Soviet troop concentrations along the border. In an address to the German people Hitler explained that he was forced to take this action, in spite of all his efforts to maintain the peace, because of the menacing activities of the Russians. Radio reports direct from the front monitored the progress of the German armies, assisted by units from Finland, Hungary and Romania.

Convinced that the campaign against Russia would be over in a few short weeks as the Red Army collapsed before the powerful blows dealt by the Wehrmacht, the German people received the news of the invasion with considerable enthusiasm, reviving spirits which had sunk to a relatively low level in the preceding months.

Kurt was excited by this new development, for with Russia defeated, the British, he felt, would be forced to come to the bargaining table. This would bring about peace without the United States becoming involved.

None of the earlier German military actions had aroused Kurt as positively as this one. He saw it as eliminating a great danger from the East, and he wanted to become part of the venture. Hartmut Hedwig and several of his closest friends had decided to move up their induction dates to one week after the end of the summer semester when their studies would be completed. In spite of his brush with the Gestapo, Kurt did not hold the incident against the German nation and was anxious to follow his friends. Joining the Wehrmacht provided a resolution to the dilemma of an expiring passport, of diverse loyalties, and the reservations held by Erika's father. Furthermore, he reasoned that by participating in the struggle against Russia, he would be able to help Germany bring about an end to the war, and thereby remove the possibility of ever having to fight against America. His commitment was not against America, but for Germany. With his mind now made up, Kurt could renounce his American citizenship with a clear conscience and become a German subject, with all the obligations which this entailed.

Erika was greatly upset over the decision, feeling deprived of a loved one whom she felt did not have to become involved in war. Kurt's life was still at risk no matter how brief the conflict in the East. Only because she believed the incursion into Russia would be over before Kurt reached the front was Erika able to resign herself to Kurt's decision. That Kurt now would be able to satisfy her father's desire for a sign of commitment to the Reich was small reason for endangering his life.

# CHAPTER V

# Disillusionment

Within six weeks of renouncing his American citizenship and volunteering for the Wehrmacht to be part of the drive into the Soviet Union "to destroy the Bolshevik menace which was enslaving the Russian people and threatening Western civilization," Kurt was assigned to an army post in Bavaria for basic training. He would later be sent to a specialized school for language instruction and the development of special communication skills before being sent to join a unit on the Russian front.

Because of the rapidity of the advance of German forces and their Finnish, Hungarian and Romanian allies into the Russian landmass, the major concern of army trainees at the time seemed not that they might get bogged down in a long war of attrition hundreds of miles away from home, but that the war might be over before they had a chance to fight. Kurt's army buddies were amused when he received a knitted wool sweater from Aunt Elsa, because they were sure he would never have a chance to wear it. In late summer Hitler, under the delusion that victory over the Russians was possible before the onset of winter, ordered substantial reductions in arms output and, failing to heed the lessons of

Napoleon, neglected to prepare his troops for a winter war. (Because of this neglect, a special appeal had to be made later to the German people for warm clothing for soldiers on the eastern front.) Aside from the threat of the dreaded Russian winter, Germany needed a quick victory, for she could not hope to match the Red Army man-for-man in a long, drawn-out struggle.

Anticipation of a quick victory in the East, as in the West and in the Balkans, at minimal cost in men and material, contributed to a distinct enthusiasm for the war; this would not have been the case had it appeared that the conflict would be long and bitter. But the recruits didn't want the end to come so soon as to prevent them from seeing any action at all and being relegated to occupation duty. Kurt realized that his language training would probably be more appropriate for occupation administration than for combat, but he, too, was anxious to be part of the great crusade to wipe out Bolshevism. Portrayal by the Nazi propaganda machine of Slavic peoples as *Untermenschen* (an inferior breed of humanity) and a peril to more civilized peoples, such as the Germans, served to diminish inhibitions on removing this *Rote Gefahr* (red threat) by whatever means necessary. (The attribution of subhuman qualities to Slavic peoples contributed in no small measure to the numerous atrocities which occurred in the East as opposed to the West.)

Within a week of the June 22 invasion the German army had pushed across Soviet-occupied Poland and reached Minsk; by mid- September Kiev in the Ukraine was encircled and captured. By November, with winter upon them, Germany and her allies held a line from the outskirts of Leningrad and Moscow in the north and past Kharkov and Rostov in the south, controlling an area half larger than Germany itself. But the

Soviet Union had not been brought to its knees, and the earlier enthusiasm in Germany began to be replaced by disappointment and uncertainty as casualties mounted and significant shortages of food and consumer products, especially soap and cigarettes, developed.

The early and unusually harsh Russian winter and the Red Army counter offensive not only stopped the invaders, but Soviet forces were able to regain approximately ten percent of the territory captured during the 1941 campaign, including the important city of Rostov. ·By the end of February 1942, total German casualties exceeded one million, including more than 200,000 killed. There were over 100,000 casualties from frostbite alone.

———————

During the first two years of the war the German people had eaten relatively well and adjusted quickly to a more limited selection of consumer goods. What was available at home was often supplemented by gifts and parcels from loved ones in the conquered lands, who sent or personally delivered when on leave such luxuries as furs, perfumes and wines from France, cheeses from Denmark, and figs and oranges from Greece. But with Russia completely lost as a source of food because of its scorched-earth policy and the necessity of drawing on domestic sources to sustain a high caloric intake for its fighting men, Germany could no longer maintain the quantity and quality of food for its home population. The meat ration was reduced, certain kinds of fruits and vegetables became scarce and wheat flour began to be mixed with corn and potato meal. Kurt, who was granted leave for Christmas, experienced great difficulty in finding suitable presents for Erika and his relatives in Hamburg, as many goods virtually disappeared from the shops.

Kurt was still in training when he learned of the Japanese attack on Pearl Harbor and the subsequent German declaration of war against the United States on December 11, 1941. He had long feared that the pact with Japan and Italy would draw Germany into a war not of its own choosing, and he was especially upset over hostilities with his homeland, however long he had feared such an eventuality. It left him no longer simply a supporter of a country trying to save the world from· Bolshevism, but the subject of a state at war with his native land. He was trapped in his predicament and could only hope that a situation would never arise which would place him in a position of having to fight his own people.

Because there was no longer any communication between the two of us, Kurt was unaware of my enlistment in the U.S. Army the day after Pearl Harbor, although he must have considered military service for me as a foregone conclusion with America's entrance into the conflict. My parents and I had been greatly disturbed earlier in the year upon being notified of Kurt's decision to join the German army, even though Germany and the United States were not then at war and we harbored no sympathy for the Soviet Union. While I did not cherish the thought of having to fight and perhaps kill my own brother, anymore than he desired to fight and perhaps kill me, I knew that the Nazi war machine had to be stopped, and on the battlefield one makes no distinction between "good" and "bad" enemies.

Because of Germany's failure to remove Britain as a contender through either a negotiated settlement or by force of arms, or to bring Russia to her knees during the year, the entrance of the United States into the conflict, the increasing severity of air incursions, and mounting casualties and material shortages, the cheer and hope which had characterized Kurt's two earlier holiday visits to Hamburg were strikingly absent this year. Germany and her allies were now no longer in a struggle merely with an increasingly isolated Britain and its empire, but, after the January 1, 1942 signing of the United Nations Declaration, with much of the rest of the world as well. Air strikes against Hamburg, while fewer in number than in 1940, were of greater intensity and claimed five times as many lives (626 in 1941 in contrast to 125 in 1940). Clusters of damaged buildings could now be found in nearly every section of the city. But there was much to be thankful for. The Blankenese home of the Schröders had been spared, neither Christina's husband, who was in the navy, nor Margaret's who was in the Wehrmacht, had come to any harm during the year, and the table for Christmas was more than sufficient. Moreover, the British flew no bombing missions against Hamburg during December.

Uncle Carl and Aunt Elsa were anxious to learn of Kurt's reaction to America's full participation in the war. "I had hoped it would never happen," Kurt confessed. "I, personally, hope that I will never have to fight directly against America. I cannot see Japan ever defeating her, but it will take a long time for the U.S. to gear up, and her forces could be bogged down in Asia for many years, keeping her out of the European conflict. I doubt if she will be able to do much before 1943, and this will give the Reich time to consolidate and defeat Russia and perhaps Britain. With the threat of Russia gone, Britain neutralized, and stalemate in Asia, perhaps some kind of an armistice will then be possible." Kurt and his Hamburg relatives toasted the prospects of a victory in the East sometime in 1942.

On December 27 Kurt traveled to Kiel to visit Erika; his visit would be brief, since he had to be back at his quarters by December 29. In contrast to Hamburg, air attacks against Kiel had nearly doubled during the year (from 15 in 1940 to 28 in 1941), claiming 282 lives as opposed to 19 in 1940. Almost all of the deaths occurred during two raids in April. Fortunately, no bombs fell during Kurt's short stay.

Although Kurt had joined the German cause partially because of Erika's parents' concern over his status, the Schneiders still held doubts concerning their daughter's continuing relationship with the former American. They had allowed a visit only after giving in to Erika's strong pleas. Although their daughter had seen Kurt in Berlin on numerous occasions during the year, this was Kurt's first visit to Kiel since the first of the year. Whatever concerns Kurt and many Germans had about the course of the war, they were definitely not shared outwardly by Captain Schneider. He felt that once the winter was over, the eastern front would be reinforced by fresh troops and, with so much territory already in German hands, a victory over Russia could be expected in 1942, long before the Americans could become a factor in the European war because of preoccupation in Asia. Kurt was well aware that he would be part of the renewed drive into Russia. Captain Schneider was also confident that the German underwater forces would be able to disrupt, if not completely cut, the supply lines to England, especially with Germany's ever-expanding submarine capacity. (German production of submarines in 1941 was six times the 1940 figure.)

However short the visit, Kurt was happy to see Erika again and she him. She pleaded with him continually to be careful and not to try to be a one-man hero when sent into combat.

As anticipated, the spring of 1942 saw Kurt among the fresh troops sent to the eastern front to bolster German forces already there. The spring offensive in the southeast was a welcome respite from the immobility and privations of the winter months and it generated new hope for an early end to the war in the East. With the entrance of the United States into the conflict in December 1941, victory over Russia in 1942 became a paramount objective of the German leadership.

Sevastopol in the Crimea had fallen by July in the new drive; Rostov was retaken and the German armies were pushing toward the Caspian Sea and the oil fields of Grozny and Baku. But the southern offensive faded as men and supplies were diverted to support the offensive aimed at the strategic center on the Volga River, Stalingrad. Stalingrad controlled the Caspian-Volga oil barge line from Baku to central Russia and the allied supply line from Iran. Its capture would severely cripple the ability of the Soviet Union to continue the struggle against the Reich.

The deeper the Wehrmacht pushed into Soviet territory, the longer were the lines of supply and communications (Mozdok, in the Caucasus and the point of furthest penetration, was 1,500 miles from Berlin), the wider the battle-front, the greater the expanse of territory that had to be controlled (an area several times the size of the pre-war Reich), and the broader the exposure to partisan attacks. In earlier advances German troops were welcomed in some of the towns and villages they passed through, and many Russian prisoners volunteered to infiltrate Russian lines to undertake clandestine missions and help "liberate" their country from Stalin's political commissars. But the abusive treatment of the people in the occupied areas, encouraged by special Army orders and a general attitude of spite towards non-Germanic peoples, undermined much of this early support and quickly swelled the ranks of the partisan forces. Acts of sabotage behind German lines were often met with cruel retribution. The anxiety to complete the campaign by any means contributed to the atrocities, as did later frustrations over the inability to defeat the Russians. Kurt could not help but witness some of the excesses elicited by war frenzy.

As the war progressed, Stalin could call upon his country's seemingly inexhaustible pool of human resources and its timeless defensive assets, the vastness of the Russian landmass and the severity of its winters, to free Mother Russia from the Teutonic invaders. Moreover, aid from the United States, promised in the fall of 1941, began to arrive through Archangel, Vladivostok and Iran. It continued to mount in spite of heavy losses from German submarines, especially on the Murmansk route.

From September through November 1942 the German army attempted to wrest Stalingrad from Soviet forces in a ceaseless, grinding battle which exhausted both men and supplies. Munitions, equipment and food were transported, partly by air, at great cost over a 1,200-mile supply line. It was during this last, all-out effort to secure the Volga stronghold before the full fury of the Russian winter made operations impossible that Kurt was wounded in the chest and left arm by an exploding Soviet mortar shell. His wounding on November 4th proved to be a blessing in disguise. He was evacuated shortly before the Russian winter counter-offensive sealed the fate of the German divisions under Field Marshal Friedrich von Paulus, who, upon direct orders from Hitler, was forbidden to withdraw his forces to more defensible positions. Again, as in the winter of 1941-42, Hitler was determined to hold every inch of territory captured instead of agreeing to the elastic defense policy favored by his generals. Cold, hungry and miserable, seemingly abandoned by their country, the German troops fought on as best they could until February 2, 1943, when von Paulus surrendered the Stalingrad salient to Marshal Zhukov. The defeat at Stalingrad, along with the Anglo-American victory over Rommel in North Africa in May, proved to be a major turning point in the European war.

By February 2, 1943, Kurt was well on the road to recovery at a military hospital near Magdeburg, far from the hell of the Russian front. He thought back on the period before his wounding when, feeling unable to give anymore, he had wished for his own death to remove himself once and for all from the agony of the battlefield. He wondered under what spell he could have been led to believe that war and dying for one's country were something glorious, the ultimate act of devotion to one's Fatherland. What nonsense! War was an ugly business, dehumanizing and demeaning, a venture which brought out the worst in man to satisfy someone's megalomanic ambitions. Yet, in spite of his loathing of war, Kurt had served with distinct bravery. In a desperate moment early in October, during an attack by a Soviet tank, he had rushed the vehicle and stopped it dead in its tracks with two well-thrown hand mines, allowing a flame thrower unit to finish off the crew. It demonstrated clearly that on the battlefield one's own survival and the survival of those on whom one depends for support take precedence over all political ideology and all concerns over the rightness or wrongness of one's cause. Kurt found that war cements a *Kameradschaft* (comradeship) as no other force can.

News of Kurt's wounding was sent to Uncle Carl, who in turn informed Erika. Both visited him in the hospital. Erika came shortly before Christmas to celebrate a pre-Christmas with Kurt, for it was not possible for her to be present on *Heiligabend* (Christmas Eve). Kurt's wounds were responding well, and it was during this visit that the two decided to become engaged as soon as Kurt was released from the hospital. They had now known each other for over two years. The previous fall, when it appeared that the war in the East would be over in a matter of months, they had agreed to wait before making a decision on a common future. But now, coming to the realization that hostilities could draw on for years, it seemed unrealistic to delay a decision in affirming their love for one another any longer.

In the hospital Kurt met scores of other young men who had been wounded on the eastern front, as well as a few from the African theater. They were surprised to meet an American in the ward, and Kurt became known as "the Ami." Here, Kurt witnessed the full range of war-inflicted wounds which human beings could possibly incur and still remain alive. Men with burned or shot-up faces, without ears, nose or eyes, without limbs, with burned or cut up bodies, with scars measured in centimeters rather than in millimeters. Perhaps the saddest case was Gerhard Jahn, who was little more than a living death. He had lost both legs and an arm; one side of his face was shot off, and he had at least a dozen scars on his body from a mine explosion. He breathed through a tube from the one lung still functioning. Every breath produced a hissing sound. It was a miracle that he was still alive. Uncle Carl, on his visit, said it reminded him of the horrible cases he had witnessed during the 1914-18 war from mustard gas blistering and shrapnel.

Kurt's hospital experience at once increased his hatred of war and gave him a renewed desire to live. His wounds were as scratches compared to the wounds of others, such as Gerhard Jahn. He realized, as his wounds healed, how lucky he really was. Yes, he would have a long scar and grafted area on his left arm and have continued weakness in the arm due to a severed muscle. He would also carry several scars on his left breast and side, but he was alive! His face, while emaciated from loss of weight, came through without a blemish. Yet, his luck meant that he would very likely have to serve again. Convalescing soldiers such as Gerhard Jahn would never have to worry about that.

It was during his hospital stay that Kurt learned about the fate of his university friend, Luther Bachmann. Luther and a friend, he was informed, were caught in Berlin distributing leaflets denouncing certain policies of the Hitler regime, particularly the harsh treatment of civilians in the occupied territories. Both were executed in August 1942 while Kurt was on the Russian front. Luther's father was arrested on suspicion, but later released. The news came as a great shock to Kurt. He had liked Luther, his frankness, his searching inquiry, his questioning of policies and directives - the very qualities that evidently got him into trouble. Kurt could understand a short prison term for such an act of defiance, but not a death sentence. There had been no act of sabotage, no killing, no fomenting of or participation in an organized revolt against the regime. The act was perhaps indiscreet, but nothing that justified his eventual fate. Certainly, Luther's accusations had an element of truth in them; Kurt had witnessed some of the atrocities himself. Luther's execution added another dimension to Kurt's growing alienation from the Hitler regime.

It was also during his hospital stay, just prior to his release, that Kurt received news that Hartmut Hedwig was missing in Russia. It was Hartmut who had drawn Kurt into many of the Nazi Party activities while the two were students in Berlin, and it was he, perhaps more than any other, who had convinced Kurt to follow him and several others in their friendship circle into the Wehrmacht after they finished their studies in the summer of 1941. It was March, 1942 in Leipzig that Kurt had last seen Hartmut, shortly before both were assigned to the Russian front. Kurt remembered him as a handsome, energetic, bright young man. His loss demonstrated to Kurt that even the mighty were not immune from paying the human costs of an all-out war. One now found few families, rich or poor, of high or low status, that had not lost a son, husband, cousin, uncle or even grandfather, as the price of the war began to add up.

Kurt was officially released from the hospital February 9, 1943, just a week after von Paulus had surrendered the army with which Kurt had fought for so long, at Stalingrad. He wondered what had become of the numerous men who had been so close to him just a few months before. He realized that had he not been wounded and had survived, he would now be among those taken prisoner.

Kurt had mixed emotions about his release. On the one hand, he was happy to leave the despair of the military hospital wards and return to a more normal life, if that was possible in wartime; but on the other hand, he felt a distinct sadness in leaving the men with whom he had lived for nearly three months. However, this was not a time for lamenting. Arrangements were being made for the celebration of his engagement to Erika in less than two weeks. Friends and relatives were informed, ration coupons pooled, and items bartered to ensure a festive affair. Moreover, Uncle Carl had contacts with several farmers in Schleswig-Holstein from whom he obtained meat in exchange for baked goods, lard and sugar. Since Kiel was an important naval base and ship-building center, with its Germania, Deutsche and Howaldt shipways, it was a prime target for the British Bomber Command and had been bombed heavily on several occasions, including April 8, 1941, and February 27/28, 1942. There had been no daytime raids since August 1941, so a Sunday afternoon, February 21st, seemed safe enough to chance a celebration. However, around 1:00 p.m., just as the festivities began, the air alarm sounded, sending everyone present to the cellar. Fortunately, no air strike ensued, and an all-clear signal was heard after 39 minutes.

The extended Schneider family was present, as well as Uncle Carl, Aunt Elsa, and their two daughters, Christina and Margaretha. Cousin Margaretha, the older of the two Schröder girls, had moved to Kiel from Emden the year before with her husband, who was in the submarine service. She knew that her husband was somewhere out in the Atlantic and lived in constant fear for his life, since Allied countermeasures against submarine warfare, including the convoy system, air patrols and sonar, were making submarine service increasingly dangerous. She wished for shore duty for him, but his small stature made him ideal for the cramped quarters of the German U-boats.

Kurt regretted that his own parents and twin brother could not be present to share the occasion with him and his wife-to-be. He thought how wonderful it would have been had there been no war and he had been able to introduce his lovely and charming betrothed to them before looking forward to a happy married life in either Germany or America.

But this was not to be. How he hoped for a conclusion to the war in the East by the end of 1943 and then the working out of some kind of an acceptable arrangement with Britain and the United States to end all hostilities! The news from the Russian front, however, indicated that the struggle there might last for many years. The days of easy victories were over. On Wednesday, February 17, Berlin announced to the German people that Kharkov, Russia's fourth largest city and anchor of Germany's southern flank, had been regained by Soviet forces. In the three months since the beginning of its winter offensive the Red Army had pushed over 600 kilometers (375 miles) from Stalingrad and was moving towards Kiev. It was not until January 28, 1943, with the seriousness of the Russian situation finally being grasped, that total mobilization was decreed in Germany. (Through 1942 much of German industry had been working a single shift and consumer goods such as refrigerators, radios and toys were still being produced in large numbers not only to moderate shortages, but to sustain the illusion that victory was still within reach.)

While there had been disappointment and uneasiness the previous year over the inability of the Wehrmacht to crush the Red Army, the failure of the 1942 campaign, after numerous early victories, seriously eroded the confidence Germans had in their future. That the war could be lost was now recognized as a distinct possibility, and most Germans probably would have been willing to withdraw from the war had there been an acceptable alternative. But it was not left for them to decide.

The pessimistic mood was clearly reflected in the conversations at the engagement reception, in spite of the presence of Erika's father. Whatever his true sentiments as a high ranking naval officer, Captain

Schneider remained cautiously optimistic that a turnaround in the war would occur in the spring. First, the Allied demand for "unconditional surrender," he felt, would stiffen German resolve, since any peace terms would be harsher than the war itself. Second, total mobilization would pull men now hiding on the farms, waiters, butlers and those in other nonessential jobs into the service or into war work, vastly increasing the size of the army and the output of war material. He had great faith in General Walther von Unruh's ability to find plenty of men to conscript. (Invested with dictatorial powers by Hitler, General von Unruh caused considerable unrest in Germany during the latter part of the war as he went from town to town looking for men to fight on the front. In factories, offices and shops he would establish a quota of men expected to present themselves for duty.) There were also those men such as Kurt, who would be returning to active duty once they had recovered from their wounds. Third, greater use would be made of labor from the occupied areas to increase production. And fourth, Germany was working on several sophisticated weapon systems which he hoped would change the course of the war. He did not elaborate on this last comment.

Uncle Carl noted the increasing severity of the air strikes on Hamburg, even as they declined in number. While there were 72 raids in 1940 and 42 in 1941, there were only 15 during all of 1942. However, the attack of May 4, 1942, had killed 77 people and that of July 27, 337 people in the heaviest and most costly air strike of the war up to that time, with over 300 bombers taking part. Over 500 major fires resulted from the raid, and, for the first time, fire-fighting units from outside Hamburg had to be called in to assist in the extinguishing effort.

"The July attack gave us some idea of what could happen if the British decided to step up their bombing attacks," asserted Uncle Carl. It was evident to him that the British had instruments that could direct them to the target, in all kinds of weather, night and day. He suspected some kind of an electronic beam similar to the long distance photo images he had seen in Berlin before the war. Captain Schneider was not helpful to him in explaining the operation of what became known as radar.

But the celebration was more than just talk about the war. Both Captain Schneider and Uncle Carl proposed toasts to the young couple for a long and happy life together. Erika's father then read several lines of verse, composed by him personally for the occasion, about the couple's courtship and then ended it with another toast, "Victory for the Fatherland."

In spite of the war and strict rationing of sugar, butter, milk and other ingredients, Uncle Carl managed to produce a wonderful assortment of cakes and pastries for the occasion. He did, however, complain about the quality of the flour. There were wine, champagne and other drinks, although not in the quantities that might have been desired. Especially good was the cherry brandy, a homemade concoction contributed by a well-wisher from the Kiel environs. The celebration was a welcome break from the stress of war.

Although Kurt had been released from the hospital, he was not yet ready to return to active duty. Because of the demand for beds created by the constant flow of casualties from the front, those who were able to complete their convalescing outside the hospital were released and scheduled for out-patient checkups.

Since leaving for the eastern front in April 1942, Kurt had seen little of Erika, and now, for the first time since their student days in Berlin, they were able to have a great deal of time together. Kurt later confided to Erika in a letter from France that this was one of the happiest periods of his life. They took long walks together, once as far as Labö. They skated and skied, and when spring came, they sailed, swam and rode bicycles. Kurt was under doctor's orders to exercise his left arm and chest muscles as much as possible, and these activities were helpful. The two also made short excursions to Eutin, Plön, Eckernförde and Lübeck. Kurt was heartbroken at what he saw in Lübeck, remembering how lovely the old Hanseatic city had been on his first visit in December 1939, before the bombings. Although militarily unimportant, the city, with its narrow streets and densely packed, highly flammable wooden beam structures, many dating back to the Middle Ages, presented an ideal target for an incendiary strike. It was perhaps for the very reason that it was burnable that it was selected by the British Bomber Command for attack during the night of 28/29 March 1942.

Because it lacked military significance, the city was poorly defended. Neither the citizenry nor the city's civil defense apparatus was adequately prepared to deal with a major bombing strike. The result was a conflagration which consumed a large portion of Lübeck. Nearly two-thirds of the city's 45,000 housing units were damaged, 320 people were killed, and many irreplaceable structures, including the cathedral, were destroyed. Although Kurt and Erika visited Lübeck over a year later, the destruction was readily observable.

Kurt could not help expressing his feelings about the war to Erika. His face-to-face confrontation with the horrors on the Russian front, the war's barbarity against civilians, his wounding, his hospital experience, the execution of Luther Bachmann, the disruption of normal human relations, and now the devastation of entire cities evoked in him strong feelings of resentment over his decision to support the National Socialist cause. He wanted to wish the war and its horrors away. The happier he was in his relationship with Erika, the greater his disillusionment; he was in constant fear that this bond would end either by Erika's death from an air attack — not even the public air raid shelters were completely safe — or by his own death in battle.

The uncertainty of everything was an unbearable strain. No definite plans for the future could be made, because in war time there might be no future. One had to live one's life from day to day. Yet, one of the joys of living is the ability to conceptualize a distinct future, and then, with all one's energies, to strive for its realization. War, because of its uncertainties, robs the human spirit of its capacity to plan ahead — to conceive a realizable future.

Kurt felt trapped. Had the war not yet involved the United States there might still have been a chance to get out of his predicament. But now, he would be looked upon as a traitor to America, and, if he were to desert the German side, he would likewise be viewed as a traitor to Germany after having voluntarily joined the Wehrmacht. As a civilian, he could have been interned for the duration of the war, but not so as a turn-coat. His options were limited. Desertion was out of the question, since it would mean death for him, if caught, and great embarrassment for Erika and her parents. Besides, trying to get out through Spain or Switzerland was very risky. His only option seemed to be to take his chances with the Wehrmacht, but to seek an assignment away from the fighting.

Another dilemma developed from a moral reawakening. Kurt began to question war as a human way to resolve differences between nation-states. Could Germany and the Soviet Union not live side-by-side in peace, or was conflict inevitable because of ideological differences or the political ambitions of one side or the other? Why didn't Germany decide to invade and defeat Great Britain before taking on the mammoth Soviet Union? Wasn't Napoleon's fate in Russia a sufficient lesson to the Nazi leadership? Was there now any way out of this war short of either total German victory or total German defeat? Was it necessary for the German cities to be leveled and the country's armed forces and civilian population decimated before there could be peace? Was it too late for any negotiated settlement?

Kurt knew that only the army now had the power to break Hitler's grip on the country. But he could not anticipate what the Wehrmacht might or might not do. With the unconditional surrender demand of the Allied powers, might not the generals now be afraid to do anything which might undermine the war effort? Might they and the Nazi leadership not be driven to continue the struggle for as long as possible, knowing that they were marked men if they lost?

At least one of the dilemmas was seemingly resolved when Erika's father, through confidants in Berlin, was able to arrange for Kurt's transfer to a unit in France with the German Seventh Army. His former unit no longer existed anyway, having been captured by the Russians at Stalingrad. Kurt eventually received orders to report to Carentan in Normandy by August 9, 1943.

On July 21, 1943, following a physical examination at the naval hospital in Kiel, Kurt left for Hamburg to spend a few days with Uncle Carl before leaving for France. Kurt found Hamburg at the height of its summer beauty, blemished only by the camouflage which covered certain areas, including the Binnenalster (a lake in the center of the city). It had been hot and dry for much of the month with temperatures reaching 32°C (90 Fahrenheit) on a number of occasions. Although the city had experienced over 130 air strikes since the first one on May 18, 1940, there had been no raids since July 7th and no massive (over 100 aircraft) attacks for a whole year. Only one aircraft participated in a raid on July 7th, and no one had been killed. In fact, not since March 3rd had there been any bombing deaths.

The lull in the air war was a welcome respite for the war-weary Hamburg citizenry, especially since the Allied bombing offensive continued unabated against other German cities. Kurt had personally experienced the May 14 attack by over 100 American Superfortresses, which killed 354 in Kiel. The raid on Wuppertal on the night of May 29/30, which killed 2,450, was only one of 43 major strikes made on Ruhr targets between March 5 and July 12th. No one doubted that the bombers would be returning to Hamburg sooner or later. Kurt hoped it wouldn't ruin his visit by happening while he was there.

Uncle Carl, too old for military service, was assigned to civil defense to back up the fire fighting units, and, while he continued to work as a baker, he was on call with every air alert. His station was in Altona, a major part of Hamburg located about seven kilometers up the Elbe River from Blankenese.

Hamburg was a high priority military target with important port, shipbuilding and aircraft manufacturing facilities, and oil refining and storage installations. Blohm and Voss, in addition to building such vessels as the super battleship Bismarck and the heavy cruiser Hipper, was a major producer of the most advanced submarines and flying boats.

---

During the early part of the war, great care was taken by the belligerents to avoid hitting each other's population centers for fear of provoking reprisals against their own cities. German naval vessels and the offshore islands of Sylt and Helgoland had been the objects of air attack, but no bombs were dropped on any German mainland settlements during these early months. Likewise, air attacks on the English and French homelands were forbidden. It was generally thought that Hitler still hoped for a negotiated peace and did not want to antagonize his adversaries unnecessarily. Germany's invasion of France and the Low Countries on May 10, 1940, ended the Phoney War, and the devastating bombing of Rotterdam by the *Luftwaffe* four days later removed many of the restrictions on air strikes against military targets within the German homeland. Several border cities, including Aachen, Möchengladbach and Cologne, were attacked during the first week after the invasion; however, the strike against Hamburg on May 18, 1940 was the first attack in force against a large German city away from the battle zone.

Although the destruction of military installations, naval vessels and war production facilities was the primary objective of these early missions, the pinpointing of widely dispersed targets from 20,000 feet in all kinds of weather, day and night, often with inexperienced crews, made precision bombing more a hope than a reality, and the accidental bombing of residential and commercial areas became unavoidable as the raids increased in intensity. The "accidental" bombing of the center of London on the night of August 24/25, 1940, was answered by a series of retaliatory missions against Berlin the following night and during the next two weeks. (The ten German aircraft participating in the mission against England had supposedly planned to hit aircraft factories and oil tanks on the edge of London, but had gotten off course.) The raids on Berlin, in turn, led to Hitler's promise on September 4, 1940, to eradicate the British cities, and there followed 65 consecutive night raids on London. The German air blitz reached its peak with the attack on Coventry on November 14, 1940. The raid greatly diminished whatever reservations the British had about bombing German civilian populations.

In a total war situation the distinction between civilian and military objectives, between battlefront and homefront, becomes increasingly blurred. The civilian population, which produces the tools of war, is as much a part of the war-making effort of a country as the soldiers on the battle line who use them. Moreover, the armaments industry concentrated in a city could be crippled just as well by annihilating the population employed in it as by destroying the separate production facilities. Whole cities make infinitely easier targets than specific installations, and results can be maximized by saturating entire areas, destroying both the military objectives located there and the resident populations. Terrorizing those who helped to sustain the war effort and undermining their will to resist were important considerations in saturation bombing strategy.

Following the extrication of its forces from the Continent at Dunkirk (May 28 - June 4, 1940) and Narvick (June 9, 1940), Great Britain had no way to bring the war home to the German people other than through her bomber force and naval units. The air war against Germany was also an important factor in maintaining British morale during the difficult period after the fall of France. Britain, therefore, dedicated extensive resources to perfecting its bomb arsenal, its delivery equipment, and attack methodology.

By the summer of 1943 Britain's air arm had developed sophisticated guidance systems, a diversity of incendiary weapons, single, high explosive bombs of up to 8,000 pounds capable of destroying entire blocks, and "window," the code name given to the bundles of metal foil strips (chaff), which, when dropped, were designed to confuse fighter aircraft and detection systems. Armed with its new capabilities, the British Bomber Command selected Hamburg for the most massive series of air attacks of the war. Little did the Hamburg population realize what was in store when it went to bed on July 24, 1943. Up to that time the city had witnessed 137 attacks, the worst of which, on July 27, 1942, involved 304 aircraft and took 337 lives. If not an attempt to obliterate a major German city, the series of attacks known as "Operation Gomorrah" was a concerted effort to cripple the Reich's second largest city so severely that it could not function.

A total of 791 bomber aircraft were utilized for the initial phase of the "Operation," which was scheduled for the night of July 24/25. Chaff was dropped over the target area to baffle the German defense system, causing flack batteries to fire blindly into the sky despite the clear night, and to keep night fighters from making contact. The unique radar image produced by the Elbe estuary mosaic of river and islands made Hamburg an unusually easy target to spot. Moreover, in contrast to such inland targets as Berlin and Munich, Hamburg did not require long flights over hostile territory. Yellow, red and green target indicators were dropped to delimit the target area.

Aunt Elsa remembered that the first air raid alert sounded some 20 to 25 minutes after midnight and was followed in a half hour or so by the thundering roar of flak and exploding bombs. Uncle Carl left immediately for his station in Altona upon hearing the initial air alert signal. Aunt Elsa, Kurt and Christina went immediately to the cellar of their home for protection, there being no nearby public shelter. (At the time of the July 1943 catastrophe in Hamburg shelters had been constructed for only about 23 percent — 378,000 people — of the city's population.)

During air raid warnings everyone except for authorized personnel was required to be off the streets. Since all homes and shops had to be left open to ensure easy access by civil defense personnel and/or to provide escape routes for those who had fled to their cellars, any unauthorized persons found wandering the streets were suspect and could be shot on sight. If found looting following an air raid, an individual could be sentenced to death. The penalty for not conforming with blackout regulations (darkening the home at night) could be as great as six months in prison.

Citizens were expected to assist in self-defense efforts by extinguishing incendiary bombs which might fall on their rooftops or penetrate into the attic. If extinguished in their early stages, the incendiary devices could be made harmless with little effort, but if allowed to burn, they could cause a major fire. Buckets of sand and water were kept ready in each household for self-defense purposes.

In spite of the thundering from the anti-aircraft barrage and exploding bombs, Blankenese seemed to have been spared the destruction that was being rained on the inner districts of Hamburg. But hope for deliverance from the fate of other areas was suddenly dashed when, a little over an hour after the initial drop of bombs, a series of powerful blasts shook the Schröder home and filled the cellar with plaster dust. The fact that the explosions stopped within a few, short minutes rather than continuing over an extended period seemed to indicate that Blankenese had not been a deliberate target. Rather, it had been bombed by only one or two aircraft which had either flown off course or were clearing their bomb bays prior to returning to their bases in England.

While the community had not been the object of a massive attack, one of the bombs that hit nearby, probably a 250 pounder, literally shifted the Schröder roof several centimeters, cracking or shattering a number of the red roof tiles, cracking and chipping plaster and breaking several windows. Kurt left the cellar momentarily to check for fire and possible incendiaries, but, when he found none, he returned to the safety of the cellar. About a half hour later the sound of cannon and exploding bombs began to lessen and gradually cease, but Kurt, Christina and Aunt Elsa remained in the cellar until the all-clear siren sounded close to 3:00 a.m.

Kurt and Christina went upstairs with flashlights to inspect the damage to the house. Plaster dust was still in the air and numerous cracks were observable, but nothing appeared to be serious. Other than for the broken windows, minor roof damage, and some cracks in the outside bricks, the outside of the house had also stood up well. "We were lucky, I guess," said Christina.

The sky was still lit up with searchlights, but more awesome, were the flames and huge clouds of smoke billowing up from Altona. It looked as though the area had been hit very hard. The major concern was for Uncle Carl who was stationed in the area of the flames and smoke.

There was a great deal of activity in the street from fire fighting units and citizens trying to assist the units. Fortunately, the bombs dropped on Blankenese had started only a few fires, as most of them had been explosive rather than incendiary projectiles. Because most of the housing units were detached, single family structures, fire fighting units were able to control rather quickly the fires that did occur. Frau Dietz's house down the street appeared to have taken a direct hit and looked almost totally destroyed. There was no fire, only rubble.

Kurt rushed out in his army jacket to see if he could be of any assistance to the civil defense units. The bombing occurred before the advent of large earth moving equipment in Germany, and the bricks, beams and other debris had to be removed by hand or shoveled piece by piece. No one had seen Frau Dietz, and it was not certain whether she had been killed by the blast or might be in her basement, covered up, but still alive. As far as everyone knew, she had been home the night before. There had been no cries heard from her cellar, but the operation of trying to clear the debris in order to reach the cellar continued. Care was taken to make certain that she was not under some of the fallen roof beams or trapped by fallen brick and concrete. Kurt and Christina helped two other members of the local civil defense unit to remove the rubble. It was beginning to get light, making it easier to see. All of a sudden Kurt heard a moan to his left. He quickly called for more light.

It was Erna Dietz, pinned in the rubble next to a portion of the kitchen wall, which had held up. She had been knocked unconscious and had remained in that state for nearly two hours before being found. Kurt and the other two men worked frantically to extricate her. Christina ran to get paramedic assistance. After about fifteen minutes, the three men were able to free the widow. The object that evidently knocked her unconscious had produced a cut and large bruise on the side of her head and she had a gash in her left leg that was still bleeding. From the pool of blood beside her, it was obvious that she would eventually have bled to death had she not been found in time. She was very weak and in need of immediate attention. Kurt quickly stopped the flow of blood with a tourniquet carried by one of the civil defense personnel. Two paramedics arrived and called for an immediate blood transfusion. Eight months earlier, after his wounding on the Russian front, Kurt had received blood from a comrade when he urgently needed it. Now he was fully recovered and welcomed sharing his blood with someone else in need, which he did. Following the transfusion in the waiting ambulance, Frau Dietz was removed to a nearby hospital where her wounds could be more fully cared for. Kurt visited her the day before he left for France to check on her progress. She hugged him and thanked him for saving her life.

Throughout the day, reports of the losses from the massive bombing of the night before circulated throughout Hamburg. Uncle Carl was not relieved from his post in Altona until late in the afternoon of the 25th after nearly 16 hours on the line with fire fighting forces. He returned completely exhausted. Units as far away as Berlin were sent to help fight the Altona fires. A thick smoke and dust cloud, rising nearly 20,000 feet, continued to hang over the city, partially blocking out the sun. Some of the fires lingered, but most of the older personnel were allowed to rest before returning to assist in putting out the more stubborn blazes.

Upon his return, Uncle Carl related what he knew about the air attack. Especially hard hit were Altona, Eimsbüttel, Hoheluft and the Northwestern suburbs, which had been saturated by a mixture of block busters, general purpose bombs, and incendiaries in a pattern designed to create the greatest fire effect. The tactic employed by the British in this raid, according to Uncle Carl, was first to release bundles of metal foil strips to confuse the defense forces, after which a series of colored marker bombs were exploded to designate the target area. Large numbers of multi-ton and smaller high explosive bombs were dropped into this space to shatter windows, raze roofs, collapse walls and create as large a field of rubble as possible, as well as to disrupt communications and fire fighting efforts. Massive numbers of incendiaries were then dropped into the accumulations of combustible debris and unprotected buildings to create as many fires as possible. The large number of aircraft insured that the area was fully saturated with bombs.

Because of the magnitude of the fires produced, civil defense, for the first time since the air war over Hamburg began, was unable to extinguish the blazes before darkness set in, even with outside help. Coke and coal in the cellars of many homes kept fires burning for weeks.

An estimated 1,500 persons perished in the raid, more than in all of the previous 137 air strikes together. Forty-three people, according to Uncle Carl, died of asphyxiation in the public shelter in the Düsternstrasse. They looked, he noted, as if they were all in a deep sleep.

In anticipation of further attacks, large numbers of people began to evacuate the city and go to the suburbs and surrounding rural areas.

Even before Uncle Carl returned home, a second raid was launched on Hamburg by American bomber aircraft in the early afternoon of July 25th. Only high explosive bombs were dropped, hitting the harbor area but not where Uncle Carl was still fighting the fires. It was the first daytime attack of the war by an American air group on the city.

A third attack was made by American aircraft in the late morning of July 26th, again against harbor installations, and casualties were light. In contrast to the RAF's night attack, only somewhat over 200 bombers participated in the two daytime raids, and the drops were concentrated on military rather than on civilian targets.

A fourth raid, involving six Mosquito bombers, occurred during the night of July 26/27, inflicting only minor casualties.

Tuesday, the 27th passed without incident, and for the first time in three days, Uncle Carl was able to return to his baking trade. Kurt, Christina and Aunt Elsa had filled in as best they could in his absence to provide baked goods for the store. This was accomplished under the greatest of difficulties as there remained repair work and clearing of the damage caused by the initial attack. It was important that roof damage be mended immediately, even if temporarily, since the wait for more permanent repair could be a number of weeks, if not months, because craftsmen were already overburdened by demands elsewhere. Window glass and roof tiles soon became costly items, but a few loaves of bread and rolls were often sufficient incentive to get the needed repairs done more quickly.

Since the 26th the Schröder household had been enlarged by two with the addition of an elderly couple, long-time friends of the family, who had lost their home and belongings, but, fortunately, not their lives, in the raid on Altona. The area where they lived near the Grosse Bergstrasse had been cordoned off, and they did not know whether there was anything left to salvage. Blankenese, down river from the Hamburg core, was considered a somewhat safer place than other parts of the city.

Fearful of still another strike that night, many people moved into the nearest "bomb safe" shelter rather than remaining at home, over-extending the capacity of a number of the shelters. Their caution proved fully justified, as the British Bomber Command dispatched 787 aircraft against Hamburg, utilizing the same targeting procedure employed in the first massive incursion, with the goal of absolute devastation by repeated attack. The planes arrived shortly after midnight, dropping their deadly cargo several miles east of the area ravaged in the first strike. Before this raid no one could conceive of aerial bombardment making a bonfire of a city. People comprehended localized fires, blasted buildings, and individuals being killed and injured, but not an inferno engulfing a major part of the city. There was no provision for such an eventuality.

The initial drop of high explosive bombs devastated roofs, blew out windows, collapsed walls, filled streets and walkways with debris, and drove households to their cellars or public shelters. With minimal self-protection activity by the residents to render the incendiaries harmless, the exposed materials ignited, and the resulting fires fed on carpeting, furnishings, wooden beams, doors, window frames, personal belongings, outbuildings, and coke and coal in basements, causing numerous small, scattered fires to become ever larger ones. The high density of the buildings and generous use of wood in their construction as well as the tinder-like quality of all wooden materials due to a long period of unusually high temperatures and low humidity provided exceptionally favorable fire conditions. The constant alternating drops of high explosive and incendiary bombs fueled the almost unhindered expansion of the fires, and within a half hour a fire storm of immense proportions was created.

The fires drew in masses of fresh air from all directions, generating hurricane-like winds of up to 165 miles per hour which uprooted trees and ripped children from the grips of their mothers. The suction effect of the storm not only strew cinders and ash over wide areas, but transported burning rafters, window frames and moldings through the air in a continual spread of the fire. Unable to comprehend the ferocity of the fire storm, many people remained in their cellars, believing it to be safer there than to risk fleeing into the unknown. The unremitting noise of sirens, cannons and exploding bombs and the jolts from near misses gave little encouragement to those wishing to wander outside. For those who were trapped by burning staircases, beams or debris or by the rapidly moving blazes, there was no escape, and they either suffocated or were burned beyond recognition. All protective measures were futile under the extraordinary conditions created by the inferno.

In spite of the most elaborate preparations and precautions, the conflagration early exceeded the capacity of the Hamburg civil defense apparatus because of the speed with which the fire spread, and fire fighting units from as far away as Leipzig and Dresden were sent to help battle the blazes. Efforts were hampered by the lack of water pressure, broken water mains, the severing of power, the breakdown in communications, the intensity and extent of the fires, and obstructions caused by rubble.

Temperatures at the center of the fire storm reached 1000° centigrade (1800° Fahrenheit), igniting and incinerating everything around. Clouds of smoke and ash rose over seven kilometers (23,000 feet) into the air, a sight which was observable from as far as 100 kilometers away. Barmbek and Wandsbek became a sea of flames, creating a vast crematorium which spared neither humans, animals nor birds. The annihilation in some cases was so complete that there was literally nothing left of some people. From the loose layers of ashes in one large air raid shelter, a count by doctors of the people who expired there could only be estimated at from 250 to 300, the exact number being impossible to determine. Thousands of others were asphyxiated and then incinerated in their cellars, or overcome by heat or flames in the streets.

All avenues of escape had been cut off before many people realized the necessity to flee. Even many of those who sought safety in the canals and water basins of the target area became victims of showers of cinders and rafters which, after being swept up by the storm and carried through the air, fell upon them.

The only ones to escape the fire storm were those who decided early enough to risk flight or who found themselves sufficiently near its edge to get out of its path. Uncle Carl, who had been relocated to the new fire scene, said that efforts to contain the fires, or even venture into the area to save people, were nearly impossible because of the great heat. A number of heroic efforts resulted in heavy losses of both humans and equipment. Uncle Carl told of a man who had saved himself from the conflagration. A Herr Keller had left his cellar momentarily to see what was happening above and outside and found himself surrounded by burning rafters. He returned to the cellar to inform his neighbors of the situation, because he was fearful that they would become blocked off if the fires continued and they didn't get out. Fearing to leave what they considered the safety of their basement, however, all but one woman refused to leave. They had survived other bombings. Why not this one? The constant explosion of bombs and shaking of the earth increased the fear of leaving.

Herr Keller decided to take his chances and left. He poured a bucket of water over his head to wet his clothing, soaked a towel which he wrapped over his head and then left the cellar with a bucket of sand in one hand and a bucket of water in the other. He threw the sand and water onto the flames which blocked the exit to the outside, momentarily dousing them, and ran into the street. He rushed toward an open square, passing many motionless bodies (some burned, some untouched) of individuals who had been either consumed by tongues of flames which had raced around the corners of buildings or overcome by hyperthermia caused by the piercing heat. With fires all around, it was difficult to determine in which direction to flee. Herr Keller momentarily froze into a stupor when he saw a woman break out in flames as she attempted to enter one of the streets off the square. She ran screaming, fell to the ground and was still. After regaining his composure, he went to her, but it was already too late to be of any help. He decided to go in the opposite direction in hope of reaching one of the canals. His vision was blurred by smoke and the continual rain of ashes and cinders, but fortunately his towel was still wet, even as his clothing began to dry out. He had to act quickly or risk being set afire or collapsing from the heat. Both exhausted and increasingly dehydrated, he pushed through the debris-filled streets, carefully avoiding any burning planks. The flames provided sufficient light as he struggled to reach his goal. Others had reached the water before him, but not realizing its depth, had sprung in and drowned. Even many of those who could swim were killed by the swirl of burning embers and pieces of wood which landed in the canals, and floating corpses and wood debris filled the water. Herr Keller and the woman who had followed him were lucky; they made their way along the canal to safety. The bodies of Mr. Keller's neighbors were later found in the cellar where he had left them; they had been overcome by heat or lack of air, and were charred.

The fire storm began to decline after four or five hours and eventually burned itself out, leaving an area of 22 square kilometers (8.5 square miles) totally devastated.

The next day the smell of roasted flesh from the 35,000 to 40,000 who perished in the fire storm filled the air. A quarter of the total Hamburg population, about 427,000, had lived in the area consumed by the fire storm, and it was a miracle that the death toll was not higher. The horror of the second massive air attack accelerated the evacuation from the city, and within 48 hours 900,000 to one million of the city's former population had fled. The Wehrmacht kept roads in and out of the city open all day on July 28 and 29 to keep the columns of evacuees moving. Kurt assisted army units in keeping sightseers from surrounding communities away from the devastated area.

Shortly past midnight on the night of July 29/30, just after the back of the fire storm had been broken, a third massive attack (the sixth altogether), involving 777 bomber aircraft, was launched against

Hamburg. Because the marker bombs were off target, the attack was unusually dispersed; still, heavy damage was inflicted on the city center and Barmbek. The death toll was relatively small, as most of the residents had fled the area during the previous two days.

Hamburg citizens began to wonder why the bombers were returning again and again, giving them no time to rest. Was there no mercy? There was nothing left to bomb! Uncle Carl was almost completely exhausted after the fifth day of bombing and had to be relieved before the final raid on August 2nd.

As if in an attempt to completely destroy the city, 740 bombers in a seventh strike were dispatched against Hamburg on the night of August 2/3, 1943. Because of a series of violent thunder storms, only about half the planes reached the target, and their bomb loads were widely scattered, some falling on areas already hit in previous attacks. Although it caused the least damage and loss of life, this final strike was probably the most terrifying; exploding bombs and the crackle of fire were intermingled with lightning and thunder above the seemingly unending noise of heavy rain, creating the illusion of a hellish inferno.

Expectations of additional attacks in the next several days continued to frighten those remaining in the city, but there were none for two months, giving the citizens a welcome pause from the death and destruction that had been rained upon them from the skies during the previous nine days.

The four massive and three medium air strikes against Hamburg involved over 3,000 aircraft and left half of the city in ruins. The large tracts of rubble and hundreds of skeletons of once functional buildings, along with the departure of an estimated one million of its pre-war 1.7

million inhabitants, gave much of the city the appearance of a ghost town. Over 35,000 dwelling units were completely destroyed; 275,000 more were damaged. The streets were left covered with thousands of bodies — mothers with children, men, old people were burned, incinerated, asphyxiated or overcome by heat, lying in every position and state of being, from fully clothed corpses to small, quiet and peaceful piles of ashes. The shelters offered a like picture. In some shelters people were sitting in a row, still, peaceful, seemingly unharmed, like individuals sleeping in their chairs, but actually killed by asphyxiation. In others, there were only the remains of bones and skulls. The dead found in streets and open places numbered 26,409; over 3,000 expired in public shelters; the remainder perished in cellars, in the water and under debris. (The Hamburg catastrophe of 1943 was the worst man-inflicted disaster in human history up to that time). The series of raids left an estimated 42,000 dead and 125,000 injured. An exact count of the dead will never be known, so completely had the fires destroyed the evidence. More people were killed in this single series of raids than during the entire eight months of the air blitz against England during the summer, fall and winter of 1940-41. Prior to the July/August 1943 catastrophe, only 1,431 had been killed in Hamburg from all previous air action.

Kurt was profoundly shaken by the enormity of the physical devastation and loss of life, and he found it difficult to comprehend that in practically a single stroke, more loss of life and injuries could be inflicted than in an entire month of fighting on the eastern front. He had experienced several air attacks in Berlin and Kiel and had been under artillery fire in Russia, but he had witnessed nothing to compare with this.

How long could Germany stand up to this awesome ability possessed by the British and Americans to obliterate the country's cities? Anti-aircraft defenses and the *Luftwaffe* had proven themselves completely ineffective in preventing the Hamburg raids or in limiting their effectiveness. Kurt saw little hope for Germany if it could not control its own airspace. The air strikes, more than anything else, convinced him that the war was lost for Germany and that it was only a matter of time before all German cities would be ravaged in the same way. At least he and Uncle Carl's family had survived the attacks!

Because of Allied control of the air, Kurt felt that an Anglo-American invasion of the European continent was now imminent, perhaps in a matter of only a few months. He was determined, as he had discussed with Erika, to use the chance of going to France as a means of linking up with Allied forces once they had established a foothold on the Continent.

Uncle Carl shared with Kurt his personal feeling that the war was lost. He no longer believed that some secret weapon could save Germany. But, in contrast to Kurt, who could view the German fate with a certain measure of detachment, he and his family, or, for that matter, the German people, had little choice other than to carry on as best they could in the face of growing casualties on both the battle front and the home front; they could only hope that the end would not be too long in coming and would come at a price they could bear. Uncle Carl, along with most other Germans, continued to see his future bound up in the fate of the German nation, wherever it might lead. He could not just flee to Sweden, Switzerland or Spain. Leaving might have been possible as late as early 1939, but not now. His survival, his very identity as a person, was ultimately linked with the survival of the German state. However much he and his family were made to suffer from the decisions of their leadership, fear of what would happen if Germany lost the war left them with no alternative but to support her, in whatever way they could, to the bitter end. One need not be supportive of a regime to be supportive of one's country! The choice before the German people was, perhaps, broader than *Tod oder Sieg* (death or victory), but the outcome would extract a heavy price.

Kurt had contacted Erika immediately after the second massive raid to let her know that he was all right. He contacted her once again on August 5th, the day before he left Hamburg for France, to say goodbye. Because of the extensive damage to the city it was not possible to leave Hamburg from the central station as in the past, so Kurt had to take a river launch from Blankenese to Harburg, where he boarded the train. The departure was a somber occasion. With Hamburg in ruins and death in the air, there was no place for laughs or smiles, only for anger and remorse. Kurt was to leave behind him a city he had come to love, a city which had taken centuries to build and which had held some of the greatest expressions of man's creative powers, turned to ashes in a few short days. He wondered, as the train pulled out of the station, whether Hamburg would or could ever be rebuilt, given the enormity of the destruction. But just as he and thousands of others had survived the catastrophe to begin the rebuilding of individual lives, why could not Hamburg rise from the ashes to become once again a beautiful and vibrant city?

And Hamburg, with a demonstration of great courage and determination on the part of its citizens, was brought back from the throes of death. Within a few weeks a large number of the evacuees returned to the city to assist in the rebuilding, and within two months most of the city's productive capacity had returned to normal. *"Unsere Mauern brachen, aber unsere Herzen nicht"* (Our walls may break, but not our hearts). To bolster morale, Germans were reminded that "this will pass, since everything has an end."

# CHAPTER V
# France and Beyond

Lingering thoughts of the Hamburg catastrophe continued to haunt Kurt on the first leg of his journey to France as his train passed through a succession of bomb-ravaged cities. The terrible devastation caused by the series of heavy air strikes directed against the Rhine-Ruhr centers of Dortmund, Bochum, Essen, Duisburg, Dusseldorf, and Cologne between March 5 and July 12, 1943, in what became known as the *Schlacht an der Ruhr* (Battle of the Ruhr), was clearly visible from Kurt's train window and it sickened him. The early morning fog gave the impression of smoke still rising from the ruins. Even if, through a miracle, Germany were still able to snatch victory from almost certain defeat, what solace, he wondered, would there be in the knowledge that it was accomplished at the price of the almost total destruction of the Reich's cities?

Ordinarily the realization of a post in France, considered to be the most desirable duty for Wehrmacht personnel because of its half-decent food, cultural amenities, numerous sensuous pleasures, black market opportunities, and absence of combat conditions, would have evoked a feeling of excitement and relief. But Kurt, haunted by the tragedy of Germany's great cultural centers, above all that of Hamburg, could not bring himself to view France as any more than a temporary haven, before it, too, would be covered with blood and ashes in the escalating conflict.

The appearance of the magnificent soaring towers of the Cologne cathedral, still standing, seemingly undisturbed, as a sentinel over the ravaged city below it, provided a brief moment of reassurance and hope just as the sight of the American flag, still flying after the bombardment of Fort McHenry during the War of 1812, must have inspired Francis Scott Key. The unfortunate placement of the central station directly adjacent to the *Dom* made it all the more miraculous that this majestic religious edifice, although damaged, had survived the bombings. Kurt had visited Cologne in August 1939, shortly before the outbreak of war, and was grieved to see the destruction inflicted on this once proud city.

After changing trains in Cologne Kurt traveled into Belgium via Aachen, which, too, had been hit hard by the bombings of the previous months. At Namur the train turned south on its way to Paris through a number of cities and places which had become household names during the first great war, among them Reims and the Marne salient.

Kurt had purposely avoided France during the summer of 1939 because he was embittered by the French treatment of Germany at Versailles and by France's interwar policies. He felt that the present European conflict might have been avoided had France not insisted on such harsh terms in 1919. He had rejoiced at France's defeat in 1940, feeling that the French were being repaid for their earlier excesses. Yet, he also distinctly remembered from his readings that the 1914-18 war had ravaged over 9,000 square miles of territory in northeastern France, while Germany had remained physically unscathed. Now he was to see France, not as a friendly American tourist, but as a member of the unwanted, oft hated, German defense forces. At least for now, France was to him a welcome temporary refuge from the frightful blood-letting on the eastern front.

As he passed through or skirted several of the important battlegrounds of the First Great War, Kurt thought back on how differently the French had fought in that earlier conflict. They had hurled hundreds of thousands of men at the invading German armies and made the Germans pay dearly for every inch of French soil they conquered, and the invaders never did reach Paris. But the French paid a heavy price in stopping the German advances, losing a large portion of a generation of young men. Kurt remembered clearly Uncle Carl's description of trench warfare on the western front — the constant barrage of artillery, the crackle of machine gun fire, poison gas attacks and the heavy losses incurred in gaining only a few hundred yards, in a war of attrition which clearly favored the defense over the offense.

Having defeated the German armies in 1918 with their defensive posture, the French brought their outmoded defense mentality into the Second World War. Placing reliance on the Maginot Line and a large land army, the French neglected the lessons of Poland, which had stressed mobility through use of armor and aircraft. The Phoney War was an expression of France's attempt to win by using outdated strategies. Rather than taking the initiative and attacking in September 1939, France and her ally, Britain, waited to be attacked and found themselves unable to cope with the new concept of warfare.

But the French defeat in 1940 reflected more than just a reliance on an outmoded strategy. The French had fought poorly. The courage which had driven them in 1914-18 was strikingly absent in 1940. France had honored her obligation to declare war on Germany if the latter moved on Poland, but she showed little enthusiasm for the struggle. World War I had regained for her the lost provinces of Alsace and Lorraine and avenged her defeat in the Franco-Prussian War of 1870-71. In 1940 she was a deeply divided people, torn by class and religious differences and Fascist sympathies, and she wasn't eager for more trouble than she already had. She lacked the will to take the initiative against Germany at a time when, with the support of British forces, a more aggressive policy might have made a difference. While France sat back waiting for something to happen, the initiative went to the Germans.

As the train crossed the Marne River along which two great battles of the 1914-18 conflict had been fought, Kurt wondered how different things might have been had France resisted with the same resolve she exhibited in 1914. Surely, he thought, the war would have taken a different course. Even had France eventually been brought to her knees, the protracted fighting and resulting carnage might have undermined support for Hitler within the army and in the German people, or, by proving that the German armies were not invincible, might have created second thoughts about the wisdom of expanding the war to the east. Instead, the easy victory against France, the only major power to fall to the Wehrmacht, created a thirst for more conquests and deluded Hitler into believing that the Soviet Union would crumble in like manner. If it took six weeks for France to fall, he thought that with a little more effort, the USSR could be toppled in 10 to 12 weeks. France's failure became a tragedy for the whole world, for it encouraged the expansionism which was to follow.

France's defeat also helped to sustain the myth of a German super race and the inferiority of other national groups, especially the Russians. This presumption, along with the belief in weapons and command superiority, thoroughly distorted the German assessment of the capacity of the Russian people and its armies to resist attack. Kurt, for one, had developed a high degree of respect for the Russian soldier, who, once his regiments had regained their balance, proved to be every bit as brave and determined as the German fighting man. Now Germany was paying dearly for her arrogance.

The train's arrival in Paris, where Kurt planned to spend a few days as a tourist before going on to Normandy to join his unit, partially enabled him to overcome his depressed state. For the first time in several years he was able to view a city exhibiting little visible damage. (Several air attacks were made on the former French capital after the fall of France, but other than a single bombing, most caused only minor damage). Les Invalides, the cathedral of Notre Dame, the Eiffel Tower, and the Arch of Triumph through which units of the victorious German army marched in June 1940, were a few of the many wonders which beckoned him.

Over 100,000 German troops were stationed in and around Paris, where they enjoyed one of the Wehrmacht's softest duty stations. The former French capital city (the seat of government having been moved to Vichy) was also an attraction for men on leave from other German units assigned to France, who sought out its museums, brothels, stage shows and fine wines. The favorable rate of exchange for German soldiers made possible the purchase of certain items not available in Germany, although the lavish buying which characterized the first year of the occupation could not be sustained as the store of many goods was depleted by the overvalued German currency. The presence of large numbers of Germans, both on and off duty, and the harsh reprisals triggered by attacks on German soldiers made Paris a relatively safe place, and Kurt and others on leave came armed with only their cameras. (When a German soldier was killed in Paris in April 1942, 500 persons thought to be in sympathy with the French resistance were deported by the German authorities to eastern labor camps and ten hostages were shot.)

Knowing since February that he would be going to France, Kurt had taken care to refresh his two years of high school French. Erika had helped him with his grammar and pronunciation. While not yet fluent, he could at least make himself understood. During luncheon at a Paris cafe he struck up a conversation with a young French woman, daughter of the proprietor. She recognized that he was not German when he slipped into English, rather than into German, when he tried to explain a difficult phrase. She asked quietly, not wishing to attract attention should her customer be an American or Canadian spy, what he was doing in a German uniform. "You're not German! What are you doing here?" she asked. "I've met Danes, Poles, Hungarians, Ukrainians and even a few Orientals in Wehrmacht dress, but never an English-speaking patron in German uniform."

Kurt knew that the Germans had rounded up men from whatever source they could, including from the occupied countries, to complement their forces, and he explained as best he could the peculiar set of circumstances which brought him to France.

She wondered how he, as a non-German, could come to support such a bestial system. In 1942 her husband had been drafted to work against his will in a German armaments factory in the Ruhr, under an arrangement worked out by Vichy Premier Pierre Laval with the German government. She claimed that tens of thousands of Frenchmen were being conscripted to work in Germany to replace Germans who had been inducted into the Wehrmacht. Her Bruno was still alive, but she was bitter to think that in this day and age human beings were being carted off like pieces of property, and forced to work as slave-laborers far away from their homes and loved ones. Could he not do something about this, something that could bring her Bruno back? She now became so emotional that Kurt was forced to his feet; motioning to other customers to remain seated, he indicated that he could handle the situation.

He could only express his sympathy. He could do nothing about the situation himself. He didn't even have relatives near Dortmund whom he could call upon to check on her husband. In paying his bill, Kurt left an extra large denomination franc note for the young woman. The incident tended to reinforce his disillusionment with the Nazi system.

———————

Under terms of the armistice agreement signed in June 1940, Germany was given control of the northern three-fifths of France and all of the Atlantic and English Channel coasts. The southern part was left unoccupied under the administration of the French government quartered at Vichy. Marshal Henri-Phillipe Petain, Pierre Laval and Admiral Jean Darlan served in various capacities as the principal leaders of the Vichy regime. All airfields and air force ground installations in the unoccupied area were turned over to the Germans and Italians, and the principal units of the French fleet were left at anchor in Toulon. The French were obliged to give no aid to the enemies of the Reich, which, at the time, were the British. The United States, which was not then at war with Germany, maintained an embassy at Vichy under Admiral William D. Leahy.

On November 8, 1942, the same day that the Allies landed in North Africa, Laval, without the knowledge of Marshal Petain, gave Germany permission to occupy the remainder of France. The French fleet at Toulon was scuttled on November 27, 1942, to prevent it from falling into German hands. France now took on a "prisoner" status, although collaboration by the Vichy government continued.

The defense of the Channel coast from Calais in the northeast to Brittany in the southwest was a task of enormous complexity. Not only was the coastline, with its mixture of rocky out-croppings, inlets, estuaries, open sandy beaches, steep cliffed headlands and two major peninsulas, diverse and highly irregular, but it was over 400 miles long.

Until the middle of 1943 Hitler could feel relatively secure on his western flank. In 1940 and for much of 1941 Britain was still recovering from its expulsion from the Continent and was itself in danger of being invaded. The disastrous commando probe of German coastal defenses at Dieppe on August 19, 1942, involving 6,000 men, demonstrated the difficulty of making an early assault on the European mainland. Conversely, the raid strengthened the Germans' confidence in their ability to repulse any amphibious attack from across the Channel. The "second front" had to come elsewhere, and the Allies selected North Africa.

With British forces under General Bernard Montgomery pushing from the east, an expeditionary force composed primarily of American troops landed at Algiers, Oran and Casablanca at the western end of the

Mediterranean on November 8, 1942, and began a drive to link up with the British Eighth Army. The operation was led by American General Dwight D. Eisenhower.

The Allied move occasioned a quick German response. German units seized Tunis and Bizerte, and a large force was sent into Tunisia. A German counter attack was launched in mid-February 1943, but was stopped after a few weeks. In a converging operation the Axis forces were slowly crushed, and by May 13 all resistance in North Africa had ceased.

Bolstered by their North African victory, the halting of Germany's eastern drive at Stalingrad earlier in the year, and growing dominance in the air over Europe, the Allies were now prepared to take a major initiative against Hitler's Reich. The next move became the subject of protracted debate. To Soviet leader Joseph Stalin, only an assault on northern France would open up the "second front" he sought to relieve the pressure on his armies in the east. Chairman of the U.S. combined chiefs of staff George C. Marshall favored a cross-Channel invasion for 1943, but a number of considerations delayed its execution until the following year. At this stage of the war there was little margin for error. A failed assault would be a serious setback for the Allies and could have delayed a follow-up attack for several years. In the meantime, Germany could, without fear, shift up to 50 divisions to the eastern theater in an attempt to cripple the Red Army, and England would have been exposed to new weapons Germany was perfecting for use against her. If it were to be launched at all, the invasion had to await the assemblage of an overwhelming force of men, planes and landing craft to ensure its success. Memories of the carnage in Flanders during World War I continued to haunt the British and caused Churchill to push for what he felt to be a less costly and more politically expedient operation, a thrust through Europe's "soft underbelly" the Balkans. Such an operation, however, not only presented serious logistical problems, but ran the risk of a fall-out with the Soviets, who had important political interests in the region. There were also others, like Air Marshal Sir Arthur Harris, Chief of the British Bomber Command, and General Carl Spaatz, Commander of the U.S. Strategic Air Forces in Europe, who firmly believed that, given time, Germany could be bombed into submission, thereby eliminating the necessity for a land invasion of the Continent.

The United States eventually accepted a compromise plan to invade Sicily in exchange for a firm British commitment for a cross-Channel assault the following spring. The Sicilian operation would help not only to clear the Axis from the Mediterranean, but might precipitate the withdrawal of Italy from the war and cause the Germans to draw units away from other areas. American and British forces landed on the southern coast of Sicily on July 10, 1943, and completed the conquest of the island in 39 days.

The relative ease of the Sicilian·campaign generated support for an early thrust at the Italian mainland. The new Italian government, established after the ouster and imprisonment of Benito Mussolini on July 25, sent out peace feelers through an emissary in Lisbon. Before British Empire forces could cross the Strait of Messina, the Italian administration under Marshal Pietro Badoglio signed an armistice with the Allies. Italy surrendered on September 8, 1943, the day before American troops landed at Salerno on the Italian mainland in support of

British and Canadian troops. Meeting little resistance, the Allied divisions swiftly established a foothold across the Italian boot.

But the surrender did not end the Italian campaign. Rome was occupied by German units on September 10, and Mussolini was freed by German paratroopers on September 12. The Wehrmacht had feared a landing farther north, near Genoa, which, if successful, could have cut off the entire peninsula. Eight crack German divisions were, therefore, held in northern Italy in case the southern incursion proved to be a feint.

From the very beginning the Italian expedition suffered from being secondary to Operation Overlord (as the cross-Channel invasion came to be known), which drew away men and supplies for the build-up in England. Units of the American Fifth Army were also later called upon to participate in the landings in southern France. Moreover, the terrain was ideal for defense, and Allied progress was slow and bitter. The Allies did not take Rome until June 4, 1944, two days before the Normandy invasion, and resistance in Italy continued until May 2, 1945, just days before the final German collapse. The significance of the Italian campaign was not in its being a decisive engagement, but in the contribution it made to Allied successes elsewhere by pinning down German divisions which otherwise might have been diverted to France or the eastern front.

---

Kurt was in Germany at the time of the Sicilian invasion and had been in Normandy only a few weeks when news of the Allied landings in Italy reached his unit. Although confident of their ability to repel any assault from across the Channel, as at Dieppe, members of Kurt's regiment were, nonetheless, relieved that the Allies had selected the Mediterranean theater and not the French coast for their next move.

A formidable system of underwater obstacles, barbed wire, tank traps, concrete pillboxes, trenches, underground tunnels and machine gun emplacements had been erected along the French coast to thwart any landing attempt. But the defenses were not uniform in strength and concentrated on those sites most susceptible to an amphibious incursion. Kurt had the opportunity to view portions of the Atlantic Wall between the battery at Fort St. Marcouf, with its huge 210 millimeter guns, and Arromanches near Bayeux in early September, and he was greatly impressed by the massive concrete fortifications and elaborate network of trenches atop the high cliffs overlooking the few beaches lending themselves to amphibious operations. He wondered at the time what awesome force and cost in human lives would be required to breach this seemingly impregnable bastion.

But to Field Marshal Erwin Rommel, the popular German war hero of North African and Italian fame in whose hands the defense of the coastal region was placed in November 1943, the preparations were far from adequate, with only the easiest beaches and ports well-defended. He pushed forcefully to eliminate the weaknesses he observed. The assignment of Rommel to the coastal command gave a distinct boost to efforts to strengthen Atlantic Wall defenses. His compelling personality was a strong motivating force among his troops. He accelerated the laying of millions of land mines, in an effort to create along the coast an impregnable strip several hundred meters deep. The system of heavily fortified artillery batteries was extended, and tens of thousands of sharp-pronged iron and steel obstacles, often equipped with explosives, were planted on the beaches and in the fields (where they were known as Rommel asparagus) to demolish incoming seaborne or airborne craft. Several coastal rivers, including the Douve and the Merderet, were dammed to form large bodies of water, often a mile wide, and deep ditches were dug in a zigzag fashion through the low areas to trap unsuspecting gliders and heavily-laden paratroopers. A mine field already extended across the Channel approaches, and a constant vigil was maintained by German submarines and patrol torpedo boats in Channel waters. In spite of the extensive preparations since his arrival, Rommel could count on only a partially completed Channel defense system to stop the Allied invaders on D-Day.

Finally recognizing France's critical importance to the defense of the Reich, Hitler, in November 1943, reversed the practice of pulling troops out of that country to feed the battlefields of the East, and by June 1944 the number of divisions in France was allowed to rise from 46 to 56. The overall quality of the divisions also improved during this period. While there was still considerable depth in the vast extent of territory controlled by the Wehrmacht on the Russian front, there would be little room to hold back a determined enemy in the West, and Hitler was no longer willing to take responsibility for further weakening defenses in France now that an Anglo-American invasion was anticipated for the spring.

---

In spite of rigorous training and exercises to keep him and his comrades in a high state of readiness, the first months of duty in Normandy were, for Kurt, most pleasurable. In contrast to those in Paris and other large cities, the people of the countryside were not unfriendly, and Kurt's knowledge of French proved an important asset in his contacts with them. The region produced an abundance of good food, and Kurt especially enjoyed its butter, cheeses and traditional drinks, apple cider and an aged apple brandy known as *calvados*. Many of the earlier attitudes that Kurt held about the French were quickly dispelled as he got to know the people better. This was rural France, not rural Yugoslavia, and whatever resistance activities existed in the cities were imperceptible here. Moreover, the weather, even in winter, was mild in contrast to Russia or even Berlin. To some elements of the German army duty here was as good as *Gott im Paradies* (God in Paradise).

The coastline of the Cotentin peninsula, with its imposing cliffs and rocky out-croppings, accentuated the great beauty of the region. The historic 11th century abbey-fortress of Mont St. Michel was a short distance to the south, and Caen, William the Conqueror's seat of power at the time of his invasion of England in 1066, was an even shorter distance to the east. Normandy had, fortunately, been spared the devastation which had ravaged the northeastern provinces of France in World War I. Paris was only three hours by train, and passes were available on a rotating basis.

With the approach of winter the mood of Kurt's post just south of St. Côme-du-Mont became more relaxed; inclement weather and the shortened days reduced the threat of invasion, which was now expected for the spring, and anticipation of a quick visit home, either for Christmas or for New Year's for most of the men, generated an unusual enthusiasm. Those from the occupied areas who had volunteered for German military duty were, of course, not returning home, but even they would be able to spend a few days in Paris.

Kurt left his unit on December 22nd with orders to return by December 29th to free others for *Sylvester.* He carried with him gifts of wine, champagne, butter, cheese and other items plentiful in Normandy, but either strictly rationed or almost unobtainable in Germany since the summer of 1941. He also was able to acquire several pieces of clothing and shoes for Erika through a contact in Paris. Because of the shortness of his leave, Erika met him in Cologne, and they traveled together by train to Kiel.

--------

The German cities continued to be the targets of relentless bombing attacks by American aircraft during the day and by British aircraft by night. After having been left virtually untouched after the July/August catastrophe, Hamburg was hit by a hundred aircraft in a daylight raid on December 13th. Kiel was struck the same day by a comparable number of American aircraft. Hamburg was not again attacked in strength until after the Normandy landings, as Berlin became the objective of a concentrated bombing offensive, known as the Battle of Berlin, in an effort to duplicate the devastating results of the summer strikes against Hamburg.

Following the initial rash of air strikes of limited strength during the latter part of 1940, Berlin witnessed an illusory calm, broken only by an occasional attack, during most of 1941 and 1942. The death count from 17 raids in 1941 was 226 and just one from four minor air incursions in 1942. The city was a much more difficult target to hit than the North German ports, not only because of its location deep within the Reich and the poor radar image which it projected, but because of the changeability of its weather.

The first major air assault on Berlin, involving 145 aircraft, was not made until the night of January 16/17, 1943. Commencing in the summer of 1943 the air attacks on the German metropolis increased in frequency and intensity and the city began to experience the devastation and loss of life which the Rhine/Ruhr and northern port cities already knew too well. On the night of August 23/24, 1943, the British Bomber Command sent 727 aircraft against the city in the biggest raid on the German capital up to that time. Fearing a catastrophe of Hamburg proportions, this and two major attacks in early September triggered a mass evacuation from the city; by mid-September a million people had fled. There was little activity again until November 18, 1943, when the Battle of Berlin was enjoined. Between then and the end of March 1944, nearly 10,000 sorties, in 19 major and a number of smaller missions, were flown against Berlin. On March 6, 1944, Berlin experienced its first daylight raid from 627 American aircraft. Nevertheless, a single major catastrophe, like that inflicted on Hamburg, was never realized in Berlin. (For the entire war there were an estimated 56,100 bomb-related deaths in Berlin. Because of the destruction of records, an exact count will never be known.)

---

Kurt arrived in Kiel to learn that both Herr and Frau Schulz, with whom be had lived in Berlin from 1939 until he entered the Wehrmacht in 1941, had been killed in the massive December 16th air strike which had devastated Charlottenburg, Wilmersdorf and central Berlin, even though they had been in a shelter. The news came as a great shock to him. He had come to look upon them as a second father and mother who had included him in their various activities, including their vacation and weekend plans. It was through them that he had gone to Bad Salzuflen, where he met Erika. They had also stood by him during the difficult anti-American period in Berlin which followed the passage of the Lend-Lease Act in March 1941. He knew their daughters and the grandchild who had been killed in one of the first air attacks against Berlin. It took all of the activities of the Christmas period and Erika's strong support to prevent him from falling into a state of despondency and ruining his short leave. Fortunately neither Kiel nor Hamburg was hit during his brief visits, otherwise he did not know how he could have handled the news of the deaths of two people who had been so close to him.

Kurt was so happy that Erika was no longer in Berlin. She had completed her studies there in mid-1942 and had remained to work as a translator in the War Ministry; however, after Kurt was wounded at Stalingrad, she returned to Kiel where she found employment at the naval base. Other than in the early months of her stay there, Berlin was probably as safe as any city in the Reich. Now that was no longer true. Kiel, of course, was always a prime target, but from the time of her arrival shortly before Christmas 1942 until April 4, 1943, the city witnessed no attacks. The devastating raid of May 14, 1943, which killed 354, more than made up for the lull in the bombing, and Kiel proved to be no safer than other large German cities. At least, in Kurt's absence, Erika could be near her parents.

Since the Christmas of 1942, when her forces were fighting on the Volga, Germany's military situation had deteriorated dramatically. In the intervening months her armies had been driven from North Africa and Sicily and been pushed back in Russia and Italy, and the *Luftwaffe* had lost control of German air space, unable to prevent the relentless air attacks on the Reich's cities. "Citadel," the Wehrmacht's last major offensive in the east, began on July 5, 1943; it lost momentum after several weeks, and within a month Kharkov was retaken in the Red Army counter-offensive, and Smolensk was freed on September 25. On November 6, Kiev, the capital of the Ukraine, fell after two years of German captivity, and in January 1944, the bitter, 900-day siege of Leningrad was lifted at a price of 632,000 Russian civilian and military lives.

Between November 1941 and October 1943 German casualties (dead, wounded and missing) on the Russian front alone had amounted to 1,684,000 fighting men, and an additional eight divisions were lost in Tunisia. Nevertheless, with over 200 divisions still intact and with Hitler confident of conscripting 1,000,000 fresh troops from industry, the occupied territories and the cohort of young men coming of age, Germany was still a potent force. Even in early 1944 Germany's major problem was not so much an inability to field sufficient manpower as the need to disperse such manpower over an area many times the size of the pre-war Reich. While a strategic pull-back would have enhanced her defensive position, it would also have exposed her allies, including Bulgaria, Finland and Romania, to the Red Army advances and denied her the significant resources of the occupied territories.

Even as conditions became more desperate, Kurt continued to hope for some end to the war, either through a negotiated peace or a realization on the part of the German leadership, as in 1918, that a continuation of the struggle was senseless. Surely, he felt, there must be an alternative to total defeat or total victory. But Hitler continued to remain insensitive to the sufferings which he had brought upon the

German people, believing that the Allies would eventually find the price of his defeat too dear, or would succumb to the arsenal of new secret weapons he was about to roll out. In his New Year's (1944) message to the nation the German leader reiterated that, in the end, there would be only "victors and vanquished, the living and the dead."

The message gave little hope for an early end to the conflict, even though Kurt felt certain that, given a choice, the vast majority of Germans would now welcome any peace which would leave them with a modicum of dignity. He believed that as individuals they had no desire to subjugate the peoples of Europe. They had been deluded by an ambitious, charismatic tyrant who had succeeded in capturing the German State and utilizing it to satisfy his hunger for power and desire for revenge. Once he had attained complete control, he could not be restrained, and the German people became puppets in his play-out of history.

They had not wanted war, yet they had supported their Führer in his victories, hoping that each would produce the peace they sought. The easy, initial triumphs had seduced them into believing that war was not so bad after all. But as success on the battlefield became more costly, as the once invincible Wehrmacht began to witness major defeats, and as the war was increasingly brought home to them through the air, their outlook turned from one of hope to pessimism and fear of the future. They felt trapped, convinced that because of the hatred that others must feel for them, the agony of a continuation of the struggle, even under an unmindful leader, was preferable to the unknown fate which awaited them should they lose the war. They had no choice but to follow their leadership to the bitter end.

Gradually it became clear to Kurt that there would be no repeat of 1918. No matter how much the German people yearned for peace, their leaders had every reason to want to shun it, except on their own terms. Because of their excesses, they feared defeat even more than did the German masses. They had been careful to implicate thousands of functionaries in their misdeeds in order to expand the universe of guilt, and, thereby, the numbers which could be counted upon to lend support out of fear of retribution by citizens and victors alike. Like scared dogs, fearing the consequences of a surrender to themselves, they were prepared to sacrifice the entire German nation.

Although an attempt was made to avoid discussion of the war as much as possible during the Christmas festivities, a total dismissal of the subject in the Schneider home was impossible. Erika's father was perceptibly worried about the course of the conflict. The submarine campaign had failed to achieve desired results and continued to be exceedingly costly. The Soviets' ability to replenish their armies in spite of massive losses was a source of considerable consternation to the German leadership, and containment of the enemy rather than defeat became the only realistic strategy in the East. The only hope was "to wear the enemy down." Captain Schneider was more optimistic about the western boundaries. He felt that the advantage there continued to rest with the defenders, who had their forces in place, whereas the English and Americans would have to transport their armies across an unpredictable body of water, exposed to the Reich's sea and air power and heavily fortified positions along the coast. In the East there were no such barriers to the Red Army.

Kurt left Kiel for Hamburg on December 27 but could visit in Blankenese for only a few hours before he had to continue on to France. Trains were slow, and because of exposure to air strikes much travel was limited to nightime hours.

Although his visit was brief, Kurt was heartened by the recovery he saw and by the fact that the spirits of the people of Hamburg had not been broken. While the city had not been rebuilt, it was now, at least, a functioning entity. Perhaps, he felt, there would still be something left when the madness of war finally came to an end.

———

As the days became progressively longer and winter gave way to spring, expectations of the long-awaited cross-Channel invasion grew. There were numerous alerts during the months of March, April and May, and the build-up of coastal defenses proceeded. Field Marshal Gerd von Rundstedt, supreme commander of German forces in France, had 837,000 men at his disposal, including about 60,000 volunteers from the masses of Soviet Empire troops captured on the eastern front in 1941 and 1942. However, the units under Rundstedt's command were widely dispersed from Holland to the south of France, and, while of uneven quality, a high proportion of the men had, like Kurt, seen extensive action. Kurt was assigned to the German Seventh Army, which ultimately was to bear the brunt of the initial assault on France.

Although the invasion zone was limited to a 400-mile irregular stretch between Brest on the southwest and the Belgian border on the northeast, the Germans could not be certain exactly where or when the attack would occur, other than that spring or early summer of 1944 would be the most likely period. The Allies organized an elaborate deception scheme near Dover, complete with an artificial headquarters for the presumed invasion leader, General George Patton, dummy guns and tanks and an encampment of real soldiers. It was intended to confuse German intelligence and cause Rommel to concentrate 15 divisions in the Pas-de-Calais area closest to the English mainland. A fleet of dummy landing craft was crowded into the waters off Dover and nearby rivers, and the area was saturated with radio traffic to give the impression of a substantial buildup. Success of the deception was vital to keeping as many German divisions away from Normandy as possible until a firm beachhead could be established.

The German defense strategy for the coastal region was a compromise between the wishes of von Rundstedt and Rommel. Von Rundstedt chose to hold back his major striking power behind the coastline until the location and size of the landings were clear and then attack with all the force at his disposal; Rommel, believing that the first 24 hours would be crucial, supported a strategy of meeting the enemy on the beaches at the low water mark and repulsing the forces before they could gain a foothold on the mainland. The compromise they worked out enabled Rommel to carry out his plan to strengthen coastal defenses, while three armored divisions were held back in reserve, subject to Rundstedt's and ultimately Hitler's command. The German dictator was confident that any landing attempt would prove to be another Dieppe, requiring a huge, costly evacuation.

The weather in May 1944 had been perfect for a cross-Channel assault, and German forces were in a full state of readiness throughout the month. When the invasion failed to come, Rommel and others reasoned that it had been postponed to coincide with the Russian offensive anticipated in June to commemorate the third anniversary of the German attack on the Soviet Union. Inclement weather and expectations of a delay in the date of the assault caused Field Marshal Rommel to leave his coastal headquarters for Herrlingen in Schwabia on June 4th. He wanted to be with his wife on her birthday two days later and left his chief of staff, Hans Speidel, in charge.

This same weather system also influenced Allied planning, and General Dwight D. Eisenhower, supreme commander of the Normandy operation, was faced with the awesome responsibility of deciding whether to delay the invasion for one day, hoping for improved weather, or postponing it for two weeks, when the Germans would be expecting the assault. Eisenhower decided to go in on the sixth of June rather than risking a later date.

The invasion fleet was not picked up on German radar until about 3:00 a.m. The small German naval force in the area, consisting of submarines, destroyers and torpedo boats, was sent out, and the shore batteries were alerted, but ordered to hold fire until the size and intention of the assault group could be determined. Shortly thereafter the batteries began to fire on the mine sweepers and destroyers escorting the invasion force, and, with the return fire from American and British warships, the battle for the Continent of Europe was enjoined. Under a smoke screen laid by Allied planes and a heavy barrage from the cruisers and battleships of the invasion armada, the first American units landed at Utah Beach, but not before thousands of Allied airborne troops had already engaged the Germans in battle during the early hours of the morning.

The mission of Kurt's unit was to defend the locks at La Barquette and the northern approaches to the bridges across the Douve River between Ste. Côme du Mont and Carentan along the major road linking Cherbourg with Paris. After supper on June 5th, Kurt started a letter to his fiancée. Other than for the posting of guards and sentries, normalcy pervaded the night. Kurt's post was alerted sometime around 2:00 a.m. when large numbers of aircraft were reported over the peninsula. Kurt and other members of his unit not on night duty jumped from their beds, dressed and positioned themselves. Such alerts had been commonplace during the past three months; it could not be ascertained immediately whether another bombing or strafing mission was in progress, such as the one which destroyed 50 locomotives in the Cotentin several weeks earlier, or if it was something much larger. It seemed highly unlikely that the Allies had called for a full-scale invasion under such poor weather conditions; however, the sounds of anti-aircraft cannon, the crackle of small weapon fire and reports of an air drop at Ste. Mère Eglise suggested more than just an air raid. Nevertheless, because Normandy was not considered to be the locus of a major invasion thrust, the air drops were viewed initially as part of a small diversion force sent in to distract attention away from the Pas-de-Calais area farther east, and the German defense forces did not react to the incursion with uniform aggressiveness.

Anti-aircraft fire, navigational errors, wind drift, bad weather and misjudgment caused by a sudden cloud bank which obscured the land below caused the American paratroopers and glider forces to be dispersed over a broad area, giving the impression of an airborne assault several times its actual size. Most of the French inhabitants of the area, fearing possible reprisals by the Germans should the air drop prove to be a sacrificial feint or eventually prove to be unsuccessful, remained in their homes.

The reaction of Kurt's immediate superior to the situation was to place his men on full alert and have them secure the area around the post in established positions. The general confusion caused by not knowing where the invaders were landing, from which direction they might be coming or in what strength kept him and other German officers from taking the initiative until the situation was clarified or the unit came under direct attack. The appropriate response, given the circumstances, appeared to be to remain within the security of known positions and to thwart any attempt to take or destroy the Douve River bridges.

Before long two captured American paratroopers were brought to the command post, giving the first concrete evidence that a major landing attempt might be at hand. Kurt interrogated the two who gave their names, rank and serial numbers. The only other information they were willing to volunteer was that airborne units were being dropped all around the area and that the German post could expect to be attacked at any moment. The prisoners were well-equipped to fight for an extended period of time before having to rely on reinforcements, and Kurt felt that the threats had to be taken seriously.

This was the first time since 1941 that he had talked to a countryman, other than American students in Berlin, and he felt strange in his role, almost as if he were acting out a movie scene. But this was dead real. He wished the roles could be reversed, that he would be a prisoner of the invading Americans rather than they a prisoner of his. But the time was not yet at hand for him to make his move, as the air assault, possibly to be followed by a seaborne incursion, might prove unsuccessful. He could not yet risk taking any initiative to help the Americans other than seeing that they were not ill-treated.

Kurt reported to his superiors the small bits and pieces of information he had gathered. From this and other sources it was known that Ste. Mère Eglise was under attack and that an unknown number of paratroopers and units from glider craft had been landed over a widely scattered area. Whether their defense position was in any immediate danger could not be ascertained. A call for assistance caused a portion of Kurt's company to move about three miles north to engage Allied forces attacking Ste. Côme-du-Mont. Kurt accompanied the patrol with his radio equipment. The defenders could expect virtually no help from the now almost extinct air arm; what aircraft remained were kept in Germany to protect against Allied air strikes there. For his part, Göring flatly refused to gamble his last remaining fighters and bombers in an attempt to repulse the Allied operation in Normandy from the air.

It was not long before Kurt's unit made contact with the invaders and a fierce battle ensued. Kurt attempted as best he could to keep his post informed by radio of the progress of the fighting until he was wounded by an exploding mortar shell which ripped open his stomach wall. He was stunned, and his immediate reaction was to hold his side. He had been wounded before on the Russian front, but this was different. It felt as though his insides were coming out. His arm also was bleeding profusely from a deep cut. Another soldier, assisting him with the radio equipment, was able to tie a tourniquet around Kurt's arm to stop the flow of blood, but before he could help Kurt with his stomach wound, he received a bullet in the head. Realizing that their position was precarious, the other members of Kurt's unit moved to another location, leaving several dead and wounded, including Kurt, behind.

Finding himself abandoned and unable to help himself, Kurt felt that his only chance for survival was to seek aid from the Americans who had engaged his unit. The approaching dawn would aid them in finding him. He called out in English, "I am an American! Please get me a doctor! Help! Help!" He repeated this several times, but there was no voice response, only the crackle of gunfire and the sound of exploding shells coming from several directions. Kurt waited for what seemed an eternity. He began to visualize himself bleeding to death on the battlefield, failing to realize his goal of being captured by the Americans and being reunited with his Erika after the war. He wondered why the Americans did not come to help him. In another desperate attempt, he again cried out for help.

The Americans did hear him, but they had to react with considerable caution for fear that the Germans were trying to lure them into a trap. They probed closer and closer. Almost falling into unconsciousness, Kurt once again muttered that he was an American in need of a doctor. By now, two G.I.s had located his position, and, edging toward him, found him in need of greater assistance than they could provide. Moscowitz ran for help to the farm house which was being used as a field hospital, still puzzled by the wounded German's command of English. He located Sgt. Schröder, whom he knew spoke fluent German, and told him what he had found. The two then returned with a medic to where Kurt was lying. Kurt only faintly grasped the fact that he had been found by his brother. Although his pain had been reduced by the injection of morphine, he was too weak to rejoice in having fallen into American hands or in being reunited with his brother. From the time he was removed from the battlefield until the beginning of the cannon barrage which battered the area, Kurt wavered between consciousness and unconsciousness. Unable to be sewn up soon enough because of the bombardment, he fell into a deep sleep from which all ministerings failed to revive him.

Kurt had come to the end of his natural existence, having journeyed into darkness in the uniform of a regime he came to despise, but of a people he came to love. He was a victim of the megalomanic ambitions of an insensitive leader who was willing to sacrifice the lives of millions of his own subjects and bring death and despair to countless others in a senseless quest for power. May ne'er again such darkness envelope the earth.

www.ingramcontent.com/pod-product-compliance
Lightning Source LLC
Chambersburg PA
CBHW070846030726
47504CB00005B/1237